When Charles Landon dies, the legacy he leaves behind has very different implications for each of his four children. For vulnerable KYRA LANDON it means a passionate encounter with ANTONIO RODRIGO CORDOBA DEL REY, a man way out of her league! What all of the Landons find through Landon's Legacy, though, is the key that will finally unlock their hearts....

Dear Reader,

Welcome to the exciting world of the Landons, and to the legacy that changes the lives of an entire family.

The idea for these books came to me when a friend and I met for lunch at a restaurant in New York. While we were waiting to be served, I overheard some women talking at the next table. They were discussing what makes a man exciting. "He has to be gorgeous," said one. "And a rebel," said another. "And not the least bit interested in being tamed," said a third. The next thing I knew, Cade, Grant and Zach Landon sprang to life inside my head. They were certainly handsome, rebellious and untamable, and when I wondered what kind of woman could possibly put up with them, their beautiful sister Kyra materialized and said, well, she'd always loved them, even if they were impossible!

In this final book in my series, meet SPRING BRIDE Kyra Landon, who goes searching for adventure and finds more of it than she can handle in sexy Antonio Rodrigo Cordoba del Rey, a fiery Latin for whom revenge is more than just a word.

Settle back and enjoy. It's been four months of love, laughter and tears as you've discovered the full meaning of Landon's Legacy.

With my very warmest regards,

Sandra Marton

SANDRA MARTON

Spring Bride

Harlequin Books

TORONTO • NEW YORK • LONDON
AMSTERDAM • PARIS • SYDNEY • HAMBURG
STOCKHOLM • ATHENS • TOKYO • MILAN
MADRID • WARSAW • BUDAPEST • AUCKLAND

ISBN 0-373-11825-2

SPRING BRIDE

First North American Publication 1996.

Printed in U.S.A.

PROLOGUE

She was not the sort of woman Antonio Rodrigo Cordoba del Rey found attractive or even likable, but that hadn't kept him from watching her for the past hour.

Crazy, Antonio thought with a little frown. What was there to look at, when you came down to it?

She was tall and willowy—far too slender for his taste, though the high thrust of her breasts and the curve of her bottom beneath the little black silk dress she wore were, he had to admit, interesting.

It couldn't have been her coloring, though it was striking. His preference was for blue-eyed blondes with skin the color of fresh cream. But this woman had skin the sun had buffed to a golden hue and eyes so gray they were almost silver. Her hair was short and dark auburn, and when she tilted her head, it framed her heart-shaped face with the color of autumn leaves.

There was even a way about her that set his teeth on edge. The tilt of her chin, the too-polite smile that was pasted to her lips... Antonio's gaze narrowed. He knew the type. Underneath the soft gold skin and the hair that glowed with red and amber fire lived an ice princess, filled with scorn and cool hauteur.

She reminded him of those museum sculptures that had little signs on them warning an unworthy public that they could look but not touch.

...*she reminded him of a time in his life he had thought he had forgotten*.

Antonio scowled and turned his attention to the woman's escort. It was obvious he thought himself one

of the lucky ones who would eventually be permitted to
touch. It was there for the world to see in the way he'd
danced attendance on her, first throughout the nonsen-
sical cocktail party that had preceded dinner and then
through the meal itself, when she'd made no attempt at
conversation and merely toyed with the chicken and
mushrooms on her plate.

It was not good food, of course. What did the North
Americans call such banquet fare? Rubber chicken,
wasn't that it? But good manners demanded one make
a pretence at eating it. The woman had not bothered
making a pretense of anything. She was bored with the
charity event, bored with her table companions, bored
with the man who'd brought her—and she didn't give a
damn who knew it.

Not that her attitude was a surprise. Women of her
class were often like that, especially the ones who knew
how beautiful and desirable they were. *Here I am*, their
cool faces told the world, *and aren't you fortunate? Just
don't expect me to feel the same, or even to pretend that
I do...*

"Antonio?"

He watched as the woman's escort leaned toward her,
said something, and smiled. It was a nervous smile;
Antonio could see that even at this distance. Surely, she
could see it, too, could sense that the man needed some
little reassurance. A smile in return, or a word.

She offered, instead, a shrug of her bare, elegant
shoulders and an almost imperceptible pout of that soft,
cinnamon-colored mouth.

"Antonio? I'm talking to you."

What a fool the man was! Why was he hovering beside
her like a pet poodle waiting for a treat? Why didn't he
tell her to stop treating him like a dog, or get up and
walk out?

There was a simple way to put a woman like her in her place. A man had to strip away that cold insolence and reduce a woman to what she really was, naked flesh and hot desire.

It was, Antonio thought with a cold smile, a lesson that brought them all to their knees.

That was what he would do with this one, if she were his.

His body tightened. He would take her in his arms, kiss that contemptuous mouth until it was swollen with desire. He would carry her out of here, take her to his private plane, and at twenty thousand feet, in the privacy of the darkened cabin, he'd strip away that black dress so that her breasts tumbled into his hands and take her over and over until she understood what it was to be a woman and not an unattainable symbol....

"Antonio! What on earth is the matter with you?"

A graceful, red-taloned hand landed on his arm. Antonio blinked, cleared his throat, and fought free of the images that had suddenly blazed to life in his brain.

"Susannah," he said, and with some difficulty, smiled at the woman seated beside him. She was golden-haired; she was blue-eyed; she was all the things he liked to enjoy—and she was looking at him as if he'd lost his mind.

He took a deep breath. Hell. Perhaps he had. Only a crazy man would waste time conjuring up such foolish imaginings about an ice princess when he had a hot-blooded woman at his side.

"*Querida*," he said softly. He took her hand in his. "I am sorry. My thoughts were a million miles away."

The blonde smiled, but her eyes were hard. "Really? I didn't think the brunette on the other side of the room was quite that far away."

"What brunette?" Antonio said, smiling. "I was thinking about you."

The blonde's smile relaxed. "For a moment I thought that you'd forgotten all about me."

"Could the tide forget the moon?" Antonio said smoothly. He moved closer to her. "I have done as I promised," he murmured. "I represented my country at the opening of the Denver Dance Folklorico Festival. Would you think it unkind of me if I suggested we leave and go someplace more private?"

He saw the little tremor of anticipation shudder through Susannah's body. She was ready for him, he knew. She had damned near been ready from the instant they'd met in Vegas—or was it Reno? For a moment, he couldn't remember. His business took him everywhere and there were always women, beautiful women who were happy to become involved even when he made it clear—and he always did—that the liaison would never be permanent.

"You are too arrogant, Antonio," a woman had told him once with something that approximated a laugh, "but then, what else could you be, with your looks and your money?"

It was probably true, Antonio thought as he rose to his feet, but there was no immodesty in admitting it. His looks were a fact of life, the only gift given him by the parents he had never known. As for his money—he had worked hard for what he had, and he owed no apologies to anyone. It was only those born to wealth, who thought it made them better than the rest of the world, who owed apologies. He had learned that a long time ago, from a woman with the face of an angel and the heart and morals of a *puta*.

Hell! What was wrong with him tonight? It was the woman, dammit, the one across the crowded room. There was nothing about her beauty that could possibly remind him of Jessamyn but everything else was the same: the look of boredom, the air of insolence.

All at once he knew she was looking at him.

The knowledge moved over his skin like a breath of flame, but he gave no hint of his awareness. Instead, he drew back Susannah's chair, helped her to her feet, shook hands with the men at the table, kissed the hands of their ladies.

And then, only then, as if it were a little gift he had been savoring, he took Susannah's elbow, turned around, and looked straight at her.

He felt as if he'd been hit in the belly with a sledgehammer. It wasn't that he hadn't expected to find her eyes on him; it was what followed. The sudden rush of heat in his blood. The desire that knotted his gut. The way everything else dimmed and faded until there was only him, and her, and the need to—to...

The woman's mouth thinned with derision. She lifted her chin and turned away sharply, and suddenly Antonio felt as if he were standing here not in this expensive, custom-tailored tuxedo but in the T-shirt and work boots he'd worn for so many years.

"Antonio, you're hurting me!"

He glanced down, surprised to find Susannah at his side, even more surprised to see the way his fingers were crushing her wrist. He loosened his grip instantly, offered a quick apology, and then he slipped his arm around her waist and led her through the room, not in a straight line but on a path designed to take him directly past the table where the woman with the silver eyes and hair the color of autumn leaves was seated.

When he reached her, he let go of Susannah, put his hand gently in the small of her back and steered her ahead of him. It was all very proper, but it gave him just the time he needed. He saw the astonishment on the redhead's beautiful face as he looked down at her.

"*Señorita*," he said politely. "Do you, by any chance, speak Spanish?"

She stared up at him, her eyes wide. After a moment, she nodded.

Antonio smiled, leaned down, and spoke in his native tongue in a whisper meant for her alone.

"Does it disgust you, to want a man like me?"

She gasped and jerked back, and he laughed softly.

"Perhaps it would make you feel better, *señorita*, to know that I would sooner take a vow of chastity than take a woman like you to my bed."

He straightened to his full height, nodded politely to the others at the table. Then he strolled unhurriedly after Susannah, through the ballroom and straight out the door.

Kyra Landon felt as if someone had just tossed a bucket of ice water over her head.

The world was full of crazy people. At twenty-two, despite her father's best efforts to keep her wrapped in cotton batting, even she knew that.

But she had never before come up against anyone as crazy as the man who'd just strutted past her.

"Kyra?"

Her head snapped up. Ronald was staring at her, his bushy eyebrows drawn together in a knot. The other people at the table were staring, too. My God, she thought, and her color deepened, if any of them understood Spanish...

"What on earth did that man say to you?"

The arts commissioner's wife leaned forward. "It had to have been something incredible," she said eagerly. "Just look at the way you're blushing!"

"Of course it was something incredible," the ballet master's boyfriend simpered. "A man that gorgeous wouldn't say anything that *wasn't* incredible. Isn't that right, Miss Landon?"

Kyra cleared her throat. "Do—do any of you speak Spanish?" she said, crossing her fingers in her lap.

The ballet master sighed. "I studied it in high school, but I don't remember a thing beyond *te amo*."

Everyone laughed. Kyra felt her heart start beating again.

"Listen, if that guy insulted you..." Ronald's narrow jaw trembled. "If he did, I'll—I'll..."

"No," Kyra said quickly. She put her hand lightly on his arm. Ronald was an inch shorter than she was and probably five pounds lighter. The man who'd just pulled that act of unbelievably crude and rude machismo had looked to be the size of a tree; he could probably pick Ronald up with one hand tied behind him. "No," she said, forcing a smile to her lips, "he, ah, he didn't insult me at all."

Ronald didn't look convinced. "What'd he say, then?"

"Ah, he said... he said he hoped I'd tell whoever was in charge that, ah, that the new center is magnificent and, ah, that he was sorry he couldn't stay for the ballet performance but that—that dinner was superb."

Oh God, why didn't I stop when I was ahead? Her audience had looked half-convinced until she'd added that bit about the meal. No one would believe that, not in a million years....

"Well," the arts commissioner's wife said with a little smile, "he would think that, I suppose. I mean, he's Mexican. Anything cooked without all that hot stuff, the chilies and what-have-you, would be an improvement."

"Spanish," Kyra said. All the heads swiveled toward her again and she swallowed hard. "He wasn't Mexican."

"Did he tell you that?" Ronald said, his brows knotting together again.

"No, of course not. I just—well, it was the way he spoke. His Spanish wasn't Mexican, it was Castilian. I studied it in school for five years. I mean, and...and..."

And I am making a complete ass of myself. But then, it was a minor miracle she was able to talk any sense at all, considering what had happened, considering that an absolute stranger who'd spent half the evening undressing her with his eyes had dared speak to her that way....

"...don't you agree, Kyra?"

Kyra blinked. "Agree with what?" she said, looking at the ballet master's lover.

"I was saying, a man that big could never be Mexican." He batted his lashes. "He was at least six feet tall, and all those muscles..."

He was more than six feet, Kyra thought. At least six-one or six-two. And yes, he certainly had a lot of muscles. You could tell, even beneath that dinner jacket. She had never seen a man with broader shoulders or with a broader chest, for that matter, and yet when he'd stood up she'd seen that his waist was narrow, and his hips. And he had such long, long legs....

The truth was that he was the best-looking man she'd ever seen. His face wasn't a pretty face, nor even conventionally handsome. The bones were too pronounced, the nose too aquiline for movie-star good looks. But it was a wonderful face just the same: eyes so blue they might have been bits of a summer sky, fringed with lashes the same midnight black as his hair; cheekbones that might have been sculpted out of clay; a wide, sensual mouth, a square chin.

She had noticed him at least an hour ago. Lots of women had; she'd seen the sly little glances shooting his way. But then, to her surprise, she'd suddenly felt his eyes on her during the cocktail party. She'd wanted to turn around, to see if she were imagining things, but she hadn't. He was too blatantly masculine, too arrogant, a man who thought he owned the world and everything in it. You could see it in the way he held himself. The blond number with him was the sort who ate that stuff up but Kyra knew better.

Besides, it would have meant being rude to Ronald, who was trying his best to entertain her despite the fact that her thoughts were back home, with her father. Charles hadn't been well for months and today he'd seemed worse than usual. But he'd still insisted that a Landon had to attend the Arts Center opening.

Kyra's mouth narrowed. And when he insisted, to try to reason was to court disaster.

"...to find our seats?"

She looked up. Ronald was on his feet; he was trying to pull back her chair and she realized, after a moment, that everyone else was filing out of the ballroom.

"Oh." She smiled broadly. "Sure. Sorry."

She took the arm he offered and let him lead her into the auditorium. The houselights dimmed, the curtains opened, and a dozen men wearing skintight leotards came leaping onstage to the beat of a drum.

"Isn't it wonderful?" Ronald whispered.

Kyra tried not to wince as a gong began sounding mournfully in the orchestra pit. "Wonderful," she said, and settled back in her seat.

She tried to pay attention to what was happening onstage, but her thoughts kept drifting to what had happened at dinner. If only she hadn't looked at the man. She'd tried not to, even though she'd known he was looking at her. But finally she'd just had to peek and when she had...

God, when she had!

That look of raw desire in his deep blue eyes had done something strange to her heartbeat and suddenly she'd felt a need so primitive it had terrified her with its intensity. She'd been even more terrified that it had shown on her face. He'd seen it. And he'd known exactly what it was. That was why he'd said that awful thing to her.

Kyra sprang to her feet. Ronald looked up, startled, and she shook her head, smiled as best she could, and mouthed that she was going outside, to the ladies' room.

What was the matter with her? To think that a man like that should hold any appeal for her was ridiculous. If she ever took an interest in a man, it would certainly not be in one who went around parading his boorish masculinity.

And yet, when she felt a hand press lightly on her shoulder, when a deep, male voice said, "Miss Landon?" Kyra swung around, her pulse racing.

Had the Spaniard come back? Was he going to tell her he'd never wanted to make love to a woman as much as he wanted to make love to her? Would she have the courage to say—to admit...

But it wasn't he. It was the manager of the new Arts Center.

"Miss Landon," he said quietly, "there's a phone call for you in my office. I—I'm afraid it's not good news."

Kyra's mind went blank. She managed to nod, to smile politely and make her way past him. She knew, even before she reached the office and picked up the phone; she knew who was calling, and why.

It was the doctor, phoning to tell her that her father, Charles Landon, was dead.

CHAPTER ONE

IT WAS a perfect morning, one that could make you forget that a raw Colorado winter was only weeks away. The early autumn sky was cloudless and so bright a blue that it was almost able to soften the dreary lines of the Landon mansion that dominated the top of the hill.

Kyra sighed as she paused beside the lower paddock and leaned on the railing. Last spring's foals were playing some kind of catch-me-if-you-can game in the meadows. Their long legs flashed and their silky manes flew as they galloped past each other. Beyond the foals, the mares grazed on the tender grass with quiet dignity.

A smile curved across Kyra's mouth. This was what made life on the estate bearable: the herd of elegant Morgans, the magnificent land rolling away to meet the soaring majesty of the Rockies... Her heart had always been here and not in the house looming above her, a house that had now become hers.

She turned, tucked her hands into the rear pockets of her jeans, and began walking slowly up the gravel path that led to the aspen grove behind the house.

There was a time she'd wondered why her father had ever built something so ugly. She knew her brothers thought it was because Charles saw all that stone and stained glass as a testament to his wealth and power. But that couldn't have been the reason. There were other houses in the foothills of the Rockies that had cost small fortunes yet still managed to capture the mountains' wild beauty.

15

When the reason finally came to her, it was so basic that she knew it to be true.

Charles had simply never given a thought to the aesthetics of Landon House. He'd have demanded the mansion be imposing in size and that it be built of the finest—meaning the most expensive—materials.

The rest of it wouldn't have interested him.

The architect had understood. He'd seen the character of his client and given him exactly what he wanted. A house that reflected its owner, a house that was show without substance, that had no heart or soul. And Charles had been satisfied. He knew nothing about hearts, or souls. Not of houses, not of people.

Not even when it came to his daughter.

Kyra sighed deeply. It seemed impossible that she had spent a lifetime living a lie.

"You're the only one who'll never disappoint me, Angel," Charles had said, right up to the end.

But she *had* disappointed him, virtually every day of her life. In her heart, where it counted, she'd never been the perfect angel he'd thought she was.

It was cooler here, in the aspen grove. Kyra gave a little shiver and pulled up the collar of her denim jacket.

Her life had changed right after their mother's death. Kyra couldn't remember Ellen Landon; she'd died when Kyra was only a toddler. All she knew was that suddenly she'd become the center of her father's existence.

"My little lady," he'd say, swinging her into his arms, "you're the joy of my life!"

But if she was his joy, her brothers were his affliction. Charles had no patience for them. He treated Cade, Grant and Zach with a coldness that bordered on cruelty. To this day, Kyra couldn't figure out the reason. She only knew that when she was five, she'd discovered the power she held.

It happened one rainy afternoon when the household was between nannies. Her brothers had been chasing each other through the halls, an activity that was never permitted. Caught up in the spirit of the game, they'd gone flying into Charles's study and somehow an urn had gone smashing to the floor.

Kyra would never forget the terror that had settled over them. She'd been terrified, too, knowing what was coming, knowing her beloved big brothers were going to be punished.

The boys didn't shrink from their duty. That night, they met Charles at the door and confessed to what had happened.

His face went cold. "Which of you broke the urn?"

The boys looked at each other. "We don't really know, sir," Grant replied.

Charles's eyes narrowed. "Tell me the truth."

"That is the truth, sir," Zach said, his voice changing pitch in the middle of a word. "We were all running, and—"

"You'll all be thrashed unless the guilty boy steps forward."

"But we're trying to tell you, Father," Cade whispered, "we don't know which of us did it."

"So be it. Who will be first?"

There was a moment's silence and then Grant stepped out in front of his brothers.

"No," Zach and Cade shouted, but Grant hushed them.

"I did it," he said.

"Did you? Or are you trying to protect your brothers?"

Grant stared at his father. "I—I—"

"You all need a dose of responsibility," Charles said through his teeth, and he herded them into the library and slammed the door.

Kyra didn't think, she simply reacted, bursting into the library after them. Charles swung toward her, his face dark, his hand on his belt, and she forced a painful smile to her lips, somehow knowing with a wisdom far beyond her years that to plead for mercy would not work.

Instead, she began babbling about her new pony and how she'd spent the afternoon learning to ride it. Slowly, the flush faded from her father's face. Finally, she asked him to come and watch her ride.

She held her breath and waited.

Charles looked from her to his sons. After what seemed an eternity, he jerked his head toward the door.

"Go to your rooms," he snapped, "and figure out how you're going to replace that urn. You're getting off easy this time."

His hand had closed over Kyra's, and it had taken all she had to keep smiling.

And just like that, she'd become the perfect daughter.

Her brothers had never guessed. As far as they were concerned, she was just a sweet little kid with an easy-going temperament who'd never realized what the old man was really like.

And why should they have believed anything else? Kyra thought with a sigh as she left the aspen grove behind and made her way toward the house. She'd found a way to make life easier for everybody and all it took was a little creative effort.

Except she'd never intended to play the role for quite so long. Her brothers were gone and she was of age. It was time—but the first, subtle signs of Charles's failing health had brought her plans to an abrupt halt.

How could she have turned on him then, when he needed her? For all his terrible faults, he was her father. And if she hadn't liked him, she had certainly loved him.

Her boot heels clattered on the steps as she made her way to the kitchen door and pushed it open. With a sigh, she crossed the room, plucked a mug from the cupboard and filled it with coffee.

Well, there was nothing to hold her back now. Her father was gone. Grant, Cade and Zach had returned to their own lives. It was time to go about hers. But what kind of life did she want? Did she want a job? A career? A college degree?

Kyra didn't have a clue. She only knew she needed to do something. Something *she* chose, for herself, by herself, with no advice from anybody—not even from her brothers.

It wasn't that she didn't love them. She did, with all her heart. It had been wonderful, having them home the week of the funeral, but it had only reminded her that, as far as they were concerned, she was still just a kid.

Cade had spent every moment—very sweetly, of course—telling her what to do and how to do it. Zach had asked a hundred times if she didn't want him to take a look at the household accounts or show her how to balance her checkbook. And Grant had done everything but pat her on the head and call her his good little girl.

It had all come close to driving her crazy but she'd gritted her teeth and endured—until the reading of the will. In retrospect, she knew it was the will that had finally tipped her over the edge.

Charles had left his private fortune, the mansion and all its vast acreage to Kyra; he'd left Landon Enterprises, his multimillion-dollar empire, to his sons.

Anger had swept over her as the attorney's voice faded to silence. Her father had done it again, she'd thought bitterly; even in death, he'd managed to keep her from the real world.

And, as soon as the attorney was gone, her brothers did it, too, giving her benevolent smiles and saying how happy they were that the mansion would be hers.

"We're so happy for you, Princess," Grant said, putting his arm around her shoulders. "We know how you love this house."

And before she could say hell, no, I *hate* it, he turned to Cade and Zach and they began discussing the quickest way to divest themselves of Landon Enterprises. *They* wanted no part of the Landon legacy but she—she was expected to jump for joy over *her* inheritance!

The realization left her tight-lipped with fury but she said nothing. What could she say in the face of such damnable male insensitivity?

And then, just as she was getting over her anger, Grant met with Victor Bayliss, who'd been their father's second-in-command at Landon's, and came back with news that put a halt to her brothers' plans to sell the company.

There were serious problems to deal with in Dallas, Hollywood and New York, Grant told Cade and Zach, ignoring Kyra even though she was in the room. She told herself it was understandable; thanks to Charles's will, she didn't have anything to do with Landon Enterprises. But the more she listened, the shorter her temper got.

Didn't Cade or Grant or Zach see the obvious solutions to the difficulties facing them? She certainly did, but no one was asking her for her opinion. No one ever had.

That was when she exploded.

"For goodness' sake," she snapped, "are you all stupid? The answers to your problems are right under your noses!"

She pointed out how easily Cade could deal with the Dallas crisis, how readily Zach could handle the problem in California. There was a moment's pointed silence and then, to her amazement, her brothers agreed.

No, Kyra thought grimly as she remembered the scene, no, they'd done more than agree. They'd acted as if the ideas were theirs, not hers. Not a one of them had thought to say, wow, Kyra, that was pretty good thinking. Thanks for your help. We really needed it!

But how could they? The big jerks had been too busy flashing each other goofy grins and putting on that disgusting display of male bonding they'd called, since childhood, the Deadeye Defenders' secret handshake.

"Damn," Kyra muttered.

She could not, she *would* not, go on being treated like a child! She would not settle into the life that was expected of her, chairing dumb committees for causes she didn't believe in, attending silly functions where she was supposed to smile prettily and pretend she was having fun...

...and where a man like the Spaniard could say the things he'd said and then vanish into the blue.

Her coffee mug clattered against the table top.

The Spaniard? What on earth had made her think of him? Not that it was the first time. Like it or not, the man had been lurking inside her head for days.

Well, it was understandable. It wasn't easy to forget such a pretentious, self-important cretin.

Impatiently, she rose from the chair, kicked it back into place, and dumped her mug into the sink. To think she'd let him get away with such rude behavior. Why hadn't she told him he was a jerk? In Spanish, of course, Spanish every bit as perfect as his. Her mouth twisted in a wry smile. According to her father, learning to converse in three different languages had been part of the education of a proper lady.

So why hadn't she hurled an insult straight back into his handsome, insolent face?

You are a toothless dog, she could have said. You are a worm. You are an animal....

Except he was none of those. That was the trouble. He was the best-looking hunk she'd ever set eyes on and he knew it. It was why he thought he could get away with eyeing women and then sidling up to them and insulting them. . . .

"Hello! Anybody home?"

Kyra spun around, her eyes wide with surprise. "Cade?"

"Squirt?"

"Cade!" She gave a screech of delight, raced from the kitchen, and threw herself into her brother's arms.

He laughed as he twirled her around. "That's what a man wants," he said as he set her on her feet, "a greeting that really makes him feel welcome!"

Kyra grinned up at him. "What a wonderful surprise! But why didn't you phone and tell me you were coming? I'd have met you at the airport."

Was it her imagination, or did his smile dim before he answered?

"Well, it was kind of a last-minute decision. Anyway, I figured I didn't need to make a formal announcement that I was coming, now that the old ma—I mean, now that Father's not. . ."

"Of course you didn't." Kyra looped her arm through his. "You'll always be welcome—wherever I live."

Cade smiled. "Thanks, Squirt."

"What are you thanking me for?" She hugged him. "I love you, you big jerk. Now, come on. Tell me all about Texas while I get you something to eat."

"To tell the truth, I'm not hungry."

"Coffee, then. I'll put up a fresh pot while you tell me what Dallas is like."

There was no doubt this time; she could definitely see his smile dim.

"There's nothing to tell. It's just a city."

"Well, did you accomplish what you went there for? Was that oil company doing as badly as you'd thought?"

"Yeah," Cade said in a flat voice. "It was a mess, thanks to—thanks to—"

"Thanks to 'the old man,' you mean." Kyra smiled and touched his hand. "It's all right to call Father that," she said softly. "To tell the truth, it's how I usually thought of him."

Cade's face went cold. "What do you mean? Did he give you a hard time, once we were all gone?"

Kyra hesitated. Now was the time to tell him, to say that there were all kinds of ways to mistreat someone, that she had been trapped in a golden cage all her life....

But Cade looked so tired. And there was a darkness in his eyes that she'd never seen there before.

She smiled brightly. "No, of course not. I was Father's angel, remember?"

Cade let out his breath. "Yeah." He smiled, then glanced wistfully at the stairs. "Sis, would you mind if I crashed for a while? I'm really beat."

"Of course. You go on up and take a nap."

"Just give me a couple of hours and then tell Stella to pile on the bacon and eggs."

Kyra chuckled. "You will have to take your chances with my bacon and eggs, little brother. I gave Stella a couple of weeks off."

"But you can't cook."

Kyra tried not to bristle. "Believe it or not," she said lightly, "you really can teach an old dog new tricks."

Cade laughed. "Old?" he said, ruffling her hair. "Old, at twenty-two?" He drew back, looked her over, and frowned. "Is that why you look different? Because you're cooking for yourself?"

"Hey," she said with mock indignation, "is that an insult?"

"I'm serious, Squirt. Are you eating enough? Maybe you need vitamins."

"Cade," Kyra said gently, "do us both a favor. Don't think for me, okay?"

It was only a teasing throwaway line, but her brother's face darkened with anger.

"What is this?" he said harshly. "The new female battle cry?"

Kyra blinked. Whatever had happened to him in Dallas, it wasn't good.

"You really do need some sleep," she said gently. She stood on tiptoe and pressed a kiss to his stubbled jaw. "We can talk when you're back among the living."

Cade sighed and shot her a weary smile. "Good idea," he said, and stumbled up the stairs.

When she heard Cade moving around, Kyra put aside the magazine she'd been reading, went into the kitchen, and laid four strips of bacon on the griddle. She hesitated, made a face, and added four more.

She'd done a lot of thinking the past couple of hours and she'd finally decided it would be silly not to ask his advice about her future. If anyone could help her with some ideas, her brother Cade was the one.

Just look at what he'd done with his own life, she thought as she began cracking eggs into a bowl. Cade had started out to be an engineer and ended up wild-catting for oil in all sorts of exotic places. He'd understand her need to shed her chrysalis and try her wings.

The Spaniard, on the other hand, would not. He'd want a woman to live in an ivory tower with a stove at one end and a bed at the other. The time at the stove might be worth it, though; he'd probably know how to keep a woman very, very happy in that bed.

One of the eggs slipped from Kyra's hand and smashed against the tile floor. She looked down at the yolky mess, shook her head, and grabbed for a handful of paper towels.

What was wrong with her? Why had she thought of that man again? It was crazy. *She* was crazy, she thought grimly as she mopped up the egg. To waste even a minute of time thinking about somebody like that...

"What?" Cade said, plopping himself down at the table. "No groaning sideboard?" He grinned. "I'm disappointed."

Kyra dropped the paper towels in the waste bin and wiped her hands on her jeans.

"I'm going to make lots of changes," she said airily. "How do you want your eggs? Fried or scrambled?"

"Your choice, babe. I'm starved. If I've eaten in the past twenty-four hours, I sure as hell don't remember it."

She waited until he'd finished everything, including two cups of coffee, and then she sat down across from him.

"Great breakfast, Squirt."

Kyra smiled. "Not bad for an amateur, huh?"

Cade smiled back. "Matter of fact, I'll have one last cup of coffee before I head to the office."

"The office?"

"Yeah. I've got to look for some papers."

Well, Kyra thought, here was an opening. It had crossed her mind that there might be something for her to do there, at the Landon Enterprises office, until the business was sold. She could learn to do things. Operate a computer. File letters. Answer the phone.

"What kind of papers?" she said.

Cade shrugged. "Nothing you'd understand."

"Try me," Kyra said, still smiling.

"Look, Sis, I know you mean well, but—"

"Why do I have to practically beat you guys on the head to make you listen to anything I have to say?"

She spoke lightly, but Cade shot from his chair. "What in hell's going on here?" he said furiously. "I've about had it with this crap."

"Well, so have I," Kyra said, just as furiously. She sprang to her feet. "Just because I'm your little sister—"

"You mean, just because you're female! Well, let me tell you something, Kyra. I'm male, yeah, but that doesn't make me the enemy! If a man didn't love a woman he wouldn't—" Cade clamped his lips together. "I'm going downtown. If Zach or Grant calls, tell them they can reach me at the office."

Kyra nodded coolly. "Yes, sir."

Cade started to answer, thought better of it, and stormed out the door.

Cade spent the rest of the week either at the office or on the telephone. Neither he nor Kyra referred to the harsh words that had passed between them.

Kyra knew something was bothering Cade. He wasn't just short-tempered, he was restless. She could hear him pacing his room at night—but then, she paced hers, too.

What was she going to do with her life?

Late one moonlit night, after she'd pounded her pillow flat, she gave up trying to sleep and slipped down to the kitchen in her long flannel nightgown. She curled up in the bay window that looked over the new snow that had fallen on the shores of Crystal Lake.

Moments later, she heard Cade coming down the stairs. He seemed surprised to find her in the kitchen, sitting in the moonlight and staring out into the night.

"What are you doing up?" he said.

Kyra didn't answer. What could she say? *I'm depressed? I'm down? I'm trying to decide if I want to study manicuring or brain surgery?*

Cade frowned. "It's late. And it's cold. You should be...you should be..."

Kyra looked at him, her brows raised, and he frowned.

"Hell," he muttered. "Do I do that a lot?"

"Do what?"

"You know. Do I tell you what to do? Am I overprotective?"

Kyra sighed. "You're not like Father, if that's what you're asking."

He drew back as if she'd struck him. "Of course I'm not! I'm nothing like him. I'd *never* be like him!"

"No. You wouldn't. You're not dominating, or unkind. And you're certainly not selfish." She smiled. "But sometimes you do like to control people you love."

"That's ridiculous."

"Maybe, down deep, you think you have to control them to keep them from abandoning you." She gave him a thoughtful look. "I wonder if it has something to do with what happened the night of your twenty-first birthday."

"What the hell are you talking about?"

"Come on, Cade, don't play dumb. It was when you learned Father had bought off that girl you were so crazy about. You were so hurt—"

"You're nuts! I wasn't hurt, I was angry."

"Losing her that way must have been awful. But someday you'll meet a woman..."

Suddenly, she knew. He'd met someone already; it was the reason he paced the floor, the reason he looked haunted—the reason he was questioning himself.

"Oh, Cade," Kyra whispered, "you've already met her, haven't you? And you don't know what to do about it."

Her brother's eyes snapped with anger. "Thank you for that brilliant, and useless, analysis!"

He pivoted on his heel and marched from the room. Kyra watched him go, and then she sighed and turned her face to the window.

Had she deepened his wound by telling him the truth? She didn't think so. Cade was hurting, but at least he was feeling like something more than a self-sacrificing martyr, which was what she'd been feeling like lately.

Hell. It was what she'd been feeling like ever since she was five years old and she'd become everybody's idea of an angel, and she was sick of it!

Kyra got to her feet. She had to do something soon or she'd go crazy! She had to experience life, to feel . . . To feel.

Does it disgust you, to want a man like me?

She came to a dead stop, the deep, husky voice echoing inside her head.

What would have happened if she'd said no, no, wanting him didn't disgust her at all? If she'd said that wanting him had terrified her even as it had thrilled her, that it had made her feel alive in a way she never had before?

Her breath caught in her throat. My God, she really was losing her grip!

A change of pace, that's what she needed. But how did you manage that when you were trapped in a house you hated, in a life you hated, with nothing more important to do than go on being the perfect little princess you'd always been?

You could take a trip, Kyra thought suddenly. You could go somewhere you'd never been before. You could see new things, do new things, meet new people. . . .

But where? Where did she want to go?

She hurried into the library, threw on the light, and snatched a leather-bound atlas from the shelf. Then she opened it to a map of the world, shut her eyes, and stabbed it with her forefinger.

Her eyes flew open and she looked down. Her finger was resting in the middle of the Caribbean.

How could you go for a vacation on an ocean?

You could take a cruise, she thought, and smiled. A cruise in the sunny Caribbean.

Kyra's smile became a grin. "Why not?" she said jauntily, and then she slammed the atlas shut, turned off the light, and trotted up the stairs.

CHAPTER TWO

EMPRESS of the Caribbean was hardly the ship of anyone's dreams. And autumn, with its potential for storms and rough seas, was not the best time to cruise the Caribbean.

But Kyra was having the time of her life.

It wasn't as if this was her first trip away from home. She'd skied in Switzerland, gone to horse shows in Ireland, and Charles had even let himself be convinced that she could spend her last semester at Denver's finest private school for girls as an exchange student in England.

But always, in her travels, there'd been her father or a chaperon at her side. And now here she was, thousands of miles from home, on a trip she'd planned, start to finish, all by herself.

Actually, no one even knew about this trip. She'd thought of calling her brothers and telling them she was going away, but what for? Did Cade or Grant or Zach phone her when they were heading off somewhere? Of course they didn't.

Then, why should she?

Stella, the housekeeper, knew. And Ted West, who oversaw the stables, had to be told, but that was it.

Kyra zipped up her white cotton skirt, then drew a pale yellow T-shirt over her head. For the first time ever, she was responsible to absolutely no one but herself.

Maybe that was why the *Empress* seemed such a dream ship, despite her dated accommodations. She had chosen the ship on impulse, from an advertisement in the Sunday paper.

Adventure! the ad had shrieked. *Excitement*! *Romance on the High Seas*!

All those capitals and exclamation marks had to mean something.

And they did, she thought, smiling as she slipped on a pair of white thong sandals. For her fellow travelers, adventure meant visits to sites of pre-Columbian settlements and museums. Excitement was wondering if the wheezing old tour buses that greeted the ship at each port would be able to get to the top of the next hill, then betting that their brakes were better than their engines as they rocketed back down to the harbor through one hairpin curve after another.

As for romance...it was sweet to watch white-haired senior citizens dancing cheek to cheek. It was also about as close to "romance" as she wanted to get, Kyra thought briskly as she screwed a pair of small gold hoops into her ears.

As far as she was concerned, the cruise advertisement had put things into exactly the right perspective. Adventure and excitement came first. There'd be plenty of time for romance somewhere down the line, but not for a long, long time.

Some women didn't agree, and that was their privilege. Lots of girls she'd grown up with were engaged to be married. She knew that most of them hadn't led lives as restricted as hers, but even so, as far as she could see, they'd simply traded their new freedom for chains of their own making.

Kyra brushed her hair, then put a white baseball cap on her head and adjusted the brim low over her eyes. Men—even her brothers—just seemed to be proprietorial as a breed. Of course, none of the men she'd ever known would be anywhere near as proprietorial as that good-looking Spaniard.

She could imagine what he'd be like! Expecting a woman to drop everything and come running if he crooked his finger, demanding her total attention be centered on him, jealous every moment she was out of his sight.

Not that there wouldn't be compensations. Kyra's breath hitched as she remembered the banked fires smoldering in his blue eyes, the harsh, almost cruel sensuality of his mouth. A man like that would know how to please his woman when she was in his bed at night. She'd lie beneath him eagerly, her lips parted, waiting for the brush of his lips, the touch of his hand....

Color poured into Kyra's cheeks.

"Honestly," she said, scowling into the mirror, "what on earth is wrong with you?"

Weeks had passed since that embarrassing night at the Arts Center. Why should she waste even a minute thinking about that horrible man? He certainly wasn't anybody to fantasize about, not unless you were interested in setting feminism back a couple of centuries.

She swung briskly away from the mirror, looped the strap of her white purse around her wrist, and made her way out of her cabin.

Mr. and Mrs. Schiller, the elderly couple in the cabin next to hers, were just locking the door. Mrs. Schiller looked up and smiled.

"Good morning, dear. Don't you look charming!"

Kyra smiled back at the white-haired woman. "Isn't this exciting?" she said. "We get to spend almost a whole day in Caracas!"

Mr. Schiller nodded. "Excellent city, Caracas."

Mrs. Schiller took her husband's arm as the little group started toward the elevators.

"Won't you join us for breakfast, Kyra? There's still half an hour before the bus leaves."

"Thank you, but I'm not taking the tour. I thought I'd see the city on my own."

Mrs. Schiller looked uncertain. "Are you sure you'll be all right alone in a strange city, dear?"

"Big city, Caracas," Mr. Schiller said, shooting Kyra a look from beneath his bushy white brows. "Got to keep your wits about you, young woman."

Kyra smiled politely. "Thank you for the advice. I'll be sure to keep it in mind."

Like all the other ships that listed Caracas as a destination, *Empress of the Caribbean* actually docked at a port called La Guaira. It was grimy and unattractive, but no one—least of all Kyra—cared. A short ride in a taxi, and she was in the center of the bustling, modern capital of Venezuela.

She'd planned her day carefully, using a guidebook and the brochures she'd picked up on ship. A cable-car ride up Mount Avila first for a breathtaking view of the Caribbean coastline, and then brunch at the Humboldt Hotel. After that, she would head down into the city and pack as much sight-seeing as she could into the remaining hours.

By midafternoon, Kyra was weary but happy. She had zigzagged Caracas on foot and by taxi; she'd seen almost everything on her list, from the beautiful gardens and fountains of La Casona to the cobbled streets and tiled roofs of the old city near the church of La Pastora. She'd even managed to spy a slow-moving sloth in the trees at Plaza Bolívar.

Now, as the sun began angling across the sky, she glanced at her watch. It was getting late, but she had at least an hour to browse the shops, and to see what she could add to her growing collection of souvenirs. Just thinking of them made her smile. Nothing she'd bought had been costly and most of the things were probably foolish but each had been fun to choose and would forever remind her of this trip in a way that expensive items from faceless hotel gift shops couldn't.

That was something her father had not understood, Kyra thought as she headed for a stretch of shops the purser had recommended. She still remembered the look on his face when she'd handed him a tiny replica of Windsor Castle that played "God Save the Queen" when you moved a switch set into one of its turrets after her semester in England.

"How...how nice," he'd said.

She'd almost explained that it wasn't "nice" at all, that it was tacky and funny and that was why she'd bought it—but then she'd thought that if she had to explain all that, it wasn't worth the effort and so she'd smiled and said yes, it was, and actually, she'd bought it for herself.

"Oh," he'd said with obvious relief, and Kyra had taken back the little castle, handed him the very proper cashmere scarf she'd bought at Harrods, and listened while he praised her for her good taste.

Nobody was liable to praise her for showing good taste now, she thought, smiling as she made her purchases. An oversize straw bag in the shape of a donkey for Stella, a papier-mâché parrot for herself, an assortment of silly T-shirts for her brothers...the gifts were fun to buy and would be fun to give.

And that was what this trip was all about, she reminded herself as she came out of the souvenir shop. Fun...

Kyra sucked in her breath as a clock in a window across the street caught her eye. Was that really the right time? She shifted her packages to the crook of her arm and checked her watch.

"Damn," she muttered, and hurried to the curb.

"Taxi," she called, lifting her hand—the hand that so invitingly dangled the strap of her pocketbook. "*Hola! Taxi!*"

Later, she would remember seeing it happen in a terrible kind of slow motion. The approaching motorbike, the grubby hand reaching out, the fingers closing tightly around the strap...

But at that moment, all Kyra knew was that a motorbike came whizzing past, something tugged sharply at her hand, and before she had time to react, it was all over.

The thief, the motorbike and her pocketbook were gone.

For a second, she couldn't believe it. She stood staring after the bike while the sounds of the street faded; all she could hear was the thump of her own heart, and then she felt her knees turn liquid.

How could such a thing have happened? This was the middle of the day, the sidewalks were jammed with people...people intent on their own business, as they'd have been in any city back home.

Big city, Caracas. Got to keep your wits about you...

Kyra spun toward a woman coming out of the souvenir shop.

"*Señorita,*" she said in an unsteady voice, "*por favor...*"

The woman smiled helplessly. "Sorry," she said without breaking stride, "I don't speak Spanish."

Kyra stared after her. Well, neither do I, she thought wildly.

Calm down, she told herself, just calm down. You *do* speak Spanish. You can find a taxi, ask the driver to take you to the nearest police station, and report this.

Or was it best to head for the ship? It would be sailing soon; would anyone realize she wasn't on board? And even if they did, would they hold up all the *Empress*'s other passengers just for her?

Of course they would, Kyra told herself, but the sinking feeling in her stomach said otherwise.

"Oh God," she whispered, and she flew back into the shop where she'd bought the shirts and the straw bag. It took time to convince the clerk that she absolutely had to take all those things back, precious time Kyra didn't have to waste, but finally she was out on the street again. She hailed a passing taxi and crossed her fingers.

She had just enough money to get to the docks. All she could hope now was that she'd also have just enough time to get to the *Empress* before the ship departed.

But she didn't. The dock where the *Empress* had been moored was empty. All that remained of her was a wind-tossed brochure bearing the ship's logo and the words, *See Exciting Caracas* blazoned across it in shrieking crimson.

Kyra stood in the deserted street, staring out over the oily water, telling herself there was no reason to panic.

Why should she panic? she thought, swallowing a hysterical laugh. Just because she had no money, no passport, no credit cards? Because she hadn't the foggiest notion where to find a police station or the American Embassy? Because, now that the *Empress* was gone, she could see just how deserted these grimy streets really were?

"*Buenos días, señorita.*"

Kyra spun around. A man was grinning at her, his two gold-capped front teeth flashing in the late-afternoon sun.

"You are 'merican, *sí*?"

His gold teeth were impressive, but so were his tattoos. A snake sporting huge fangs writhed on one arm; a pierced heart dripped crimson blood down the other.

Kyra cleared her throat. "I—I..."

I, what? Why was she stammering? So he had gold teeth. So he had tattoos. So what? She was on her own now; she wasn't in a place where she'd be rubbing shoulders with men in tuxedos. Gold teeth and tattoos, she thought firmly, did not mean he was a bad person!

And so she smiled politely. "Yes," she said, "I am. Could you tell me where I can find the American Embassy?"

"Ah, but the embassy is closed at this hour, señorita." Gold Teeth frowned. "Is there some difficulty?"

Kyra nodded. "I've been robbed."

Gold Teeth gasped. "Robbed? By one of my countrymen?" He clucked in sympathy. "That is most unfortunate. You must report this to the *policía* at once."

Kyra managed a slight smile. "I would, if I knew where to find the nearest station. I don't suppose you'd know..."

He turned and pointed toward a dark alley. "Of course. It is right through there."

Kyra peered over his shoulder. The alley wasn't just dark, it was almost black. She couldn't see more than a couple of feet into it.

"Where?" she said. "I don't see..."

"Ah, you must go to the end, *señorita*. And then there is a right turn, and a left, and another left..." Gold Teeth looked at her. "Come, *señorita*. I will take you there myself."

Kyra looked at the alley, then at her would-be rescuer. Suddenly, old Mr. Schiller's voice rang in her ears.

Got to keep your wits about you... it said.

She took a step back. "No," she said politely, "thank you very much for offering, but—"

"*Señorita.*" Gold Teeth smiled slyly, shuffled closer, and breathed cheap whiskey into her face. "You have no money, yes? An' no man to help you."

"I'll be fine, *señor*. I am grateful, but—"

His hand shot out and clamped around her wrist.

"Be nice," he said, "an' I be nice, too. Otherwise—"

"Let me go," Kyra demanded, twisting furiously against him.

Gold Teeth laughed as if she'd made a wonderful joke. "Sure. I let you go. But first—"

"I would suggest you take the lady's advice, *compadre*."

The voice came from behind her. It was male, deeply pitched, and though it was almost lazy in tone, there was no mistaking the authority in it.

Gold Teeth almost snarled with annoyance.

"This is not your business, man."

"I have made it my business. Let go of the woman and I will permit you to leave here in peace."

Gold Teeth threw back his head and laughed. "Oh, I am shaking with fear."

The stranger's voice hardened. "For the last time, let her go."

"Why?" Gold Teeth's smile twisted into an obscene grin and he nodded his head slyly. "Now I unnerstand. You want her for yourself." Kyra stumbled as he shoved her aside. "Come and get her, then," he said, and suddenly there was a knife glinting in his hand.

The man shot past Kyra with the swiftness of a jungle cat. There was a blur of motion, a thud, a groan. The knife went flying and Gold Teeth fell to his knees, swayed there, then sprawled flat on his face.

Twice in one day, Kyra thought hysterically, twice in one *hour* something incredible had happened too fast for her to see!

Her rescuer bent, lifted Gold Teeth to his feet. He said something in Spanish Kyra couldn't understand but Gold

Teeth certainly did. Even though he was swaying unsteadily, he gulped, nodded, and took off.

Kyra dragged air deep into her lungs and took a step toward her rescuer, who was standing with his back to her and his hands on his hips, watching her assailant as he vanished into the alley.

My God, she thought with admiration, he wasn't even breathing hard.

With a shaking hand, she took off her baseball cap and ran her fingers through her hair.

"*Señor*," she said, trying to keep her voice steady. "*Señor*, I am so grateful . . ."

"*Señorita*," the man said sternly, "this man was a— a *marrano* . . ." He shook his head. "Do you speak any Spanish?"

Kyra went very still. No, she thought, no, it couldn't be.

Her heart rose into her throat. She watched as her rescuer dusted off his hands and then turned toward her.

"He was, you would say, a pig. So you will understand when I tell you—"

Cristo!

Antonio Rodrigo Cordoba del Rey stared at the woman. No. No, it couldn't be!

His sapphire eyes turned almost black with shock as he stared at her, at the face he had not managed to forget, despite the weeks that had gone by since he had first seen it.

He saw her throat work convulsively.

"No," she whispered, "no! I don't believe it."

Antonio rubbed his hands over his eyes but it didn't help. When he looked again, she was still standing there in front of him, dressed in a skirt and sandals and a T-shirt instead of in a little slip of black silk, but there was no mistaking her identity.

This was the woman who had reduced him to such foolishness that night in Denver. He had thought of her a dozen times since then, never without his gut knotting with anger, always assuring himself that the only saving grace in the whole damned scenario was that he would never, ever, have to see her again....

Yet, here she was. *Por Dios*, how could such a thing have happened?

He took a step toward her, his fists knotted as he fought for self-control.

"What in hell are you doing here?" he demanded.

The woman's head snapped back as if he'd struck her.

"What am *I* doing here?" she said. Her voice was breathy, as if she'd been running. She moved closer, her head tilted up, her eyes locked on his. "What do you mean, what am *I* doing here?"

Antonio's eyes narrowed. "I cannot believe this. What have I done that the gods should drop you into my lap a second time?"

Kyra stared at him. The arrogant, insolent, self-centered jerk...

"My sentiments precisely," she sputtered. "Suffering through one encounter with you was enough for a lifetime. No woman should have to endure your presence twice!"

A dark flush crept across his face. "You should count yourself fortunate for this second test of your stamina, *señorita*. Had it not occurred, you would have found yourself involved in a much more interesting adventure with your charming friend!"

"That—that creature was not my 'friend'!"

A chill smile curved over Antonio's mouth. "You should choose more carefully when you decide to 'play with the natives'."

Kyra's eyes turned from silver to smoke. "I do not have to stand here and listen to these insults!"

"You most certainly do not."

"Fine."

She spun away, but the memory of his disdainful little smile, even of the way he was standing, with his arms crossed over his chest, enraged her. All that smug male superiority...how dare he? She took a breath, turned, and faced him again.

"Has anyone ever told you that you are, without question, the most...the most insufferable human being imaginable?"

One midnight black eyebrow rose in lazy amusement.

"And to think that moments ago you were almost on your knees to me with gratitude," he drawled.

Kyra's color heightened. "You only wish!"

The smile faded from his lips. "My only wish is that I awaken in a few seconds and find out that you have once again been nothing but a bad dream!"

"Really?" Kyra purred. "Have I been in your dreams, *señor*?"

Antonio flushed. Dammit, why was he letting her draw him into this ridiculous battle of words? As it was, he had made a stupid slip. He *had* been dreaming of her ever since that night they'd first encountered each other; incredible, X-rated dreams that were ridiculous when you considered that he was not a man who needed to waste his sexual energies in fantasies and that this tart-tongued, mean-tempered American was the last woman he'd ever want in his bed.

"Well?"

He looked at her. Her head was tilted at a slight angle and she was watching him with catlike intensity.

He took a step toward her. "I see that you are a woman who likes to live dangerously. But I must warn you, señorita, that it would be reckless to push a man like me too far. You might not escape as easily as you did a few moments ago."

Kyra's heart kicked against her ribs. He was right. Not about the incident with Gold Teeth but about what was happening now. You didn't tease a man like this; you didn't dangle bait and wait to see if he'd snap it up. She remembered all too clearly the way he'd watched her that night, the sexual heat that had smoldered between them.

"Perhaps it is I who should have asked that question of you, *señorita*."

She looked up. He had moved closer to her; they were standing barely a whisper apart. She swallowed, then cleared her throat.

"What—what question?"

"About dreams," he said. His smile was sexy and dangerous. "Have *you* dreamed of *me*, *señorita*?"

Kyra stepped back. "Never," she said, her chin lifted. "Unless I'm in the middle of a very bad one right now."

Antonio's nostrils flared. He reached out and clasped her by the shoulders.

"Do you feel the bite of my fingers? I promise you, what is happening is no dream."

Yes. Yes, she could feel the bite of his fingers, feel the heat of his touch. She could see that his eyes were the color of sapphires, that there was a small, almost invisible scar angled across his jaw; she could smell his scent, equal parts sun and sea and raw male anger.

He looked down at her, his eyes dark, and then he drew her forward against his hard body.

"We are both here. In the flesh—isn't that what you Americans say? And just so there's no further confusion in your mind, I will prove it to you."

And before Kyra could stop him, he gathered her into his arms and kissed her.

CHAPTER THREE

ANTONIO sat behind his desk, his arms crossed over his chest. He'd tilted his leather-and-oak chair back on its legs and now he was scowling at the ceiling instead of at the door, which was what he'd been doing for the last five minutes or for however long it had taken him to count silently to a hundred in Spanish, in English, and finally even in the Indio dialect he'd spent most of his adult life trying to forget.

It hadn't helped. His patience, never his strongest asset, he had to admit, was wearing thin. But then, why wouldn't it? His scowl deepened as he leaned forward and let the front legs of his chair bang against the wide-planked teak floor.

How much time could a woman spend in the ladies' room, for God's sake?

Antonio rose to his feet, stalked to the window, and turned his scowl on the rain. Damn the weather, anyhow. He'd been away so long he'd almost forgotten the cloud-bursts that were so common to the tropics. If only it had started to rain sooner. Maybe then none of this would have happened. Maybe his secretary wouldn't have looked outside and seen a woman—a *turista*, she'd said—being harassed just outside the door.

"Shall I call the police?" Consuelo had asked.

Antonio had hesitated. Calling the police seemed like overkill. This wouldn't be the first drunken sailor to make a pest of himself on the docks.

And so he'd sighed with resignation at the interruption, risen from his desk, and assured Consuelo that he would deal with the problem.

And so he had, he thought now, suppressing the faintest smile of satisfaction. It was a long time since he'd used his fists, but then, disarming a fool with a knife was not a skill one forgot.

His smile turned into a frown as he remembered how the smile of gratitude disappeared from the *turista*'s lips when she'd realized who it was that had saved her beautiful neck. Did she really think she was the only one who was appalled by this unbelievable coincidence? To find himself face-to-face with the woman again...

Not in a million years would he have imagined such a thing!

Antonio turned away from the window. One good thing, at least, had come of this encounter.

He knew with certainty that he would not be bothered by unwanted images of the American's coldly beautiful face any longer.

Inconceivable as it seemed, her face had haunted him, but that was over now. He'd seen her again and the only emotion he'd felt had been disbelief. Better still, he'd given her a taste of her own medicine. He'd kissed her, had the satisfaction of knowing that he could make her tremble with desire for a man like him....

Who was he kidding? She hadn't trembled. The kiss had only lasted for an instant but it had been long enough for him to feel her go rigid with shock in his arms.

And then the skies had opened up and Consuelo had stuck her nose where it didn't belong yet a second time. She'd come dashing out into the street, shot him a look of fierce remonstration, and before he could stop her, she'd put her arm around the woman and rushed her inside.

Now here he was, cooling his heels, a captive in his own office, dammit, waiting for the American to deign to reappear so he could call her a taxi and send her back to wherever she'd come from, so he could get back to work and maybe, just maybe, tie up his business in Caracas so he could get out of here and be back on San Sebastian Island tonight.

He shot back his cuff, glared at his watch, then marched to the door and yanked it open.

"Consuelo," he bellowed.

His secretary looked up from her desk, her expression impassive.

"*Sí, señor*?"

Antonio folded his arms over his chest. "Where is she?"

"She is still in the ladies' room, *señor*."

"Does she think I have the day to waste?"

"I am certain she will only be another few minutes. She asked for a comb and—"

"And you obliged? What for? Are you her maid?"

Consuelo's tone grew cool. "The *señorita* has been through a most unfortunate experience, *señor*. I should think any decent human being would feel some compassion for her."

Antonio opened his mouth, then closed it again. The rebuke was unsubtle, but then, lack of subtlety was one of his secretary's assets. Consuelo was old enough to be his mother; she had been with him for ten years, and whenever he needed to be brought back to size—as, he supposed, he might on extremely rare occasions—she was the only one with the courage to do it.

"She has had a difficult time, Señor del Rey," Consuelo added softly.

Antonio's mouth hardened. "Perhaps she has also learned a lesson. The world and its inhabitants are not toys put here for her amusement."

He turned and slammed the door behind him before
Consuelo could respond. Then he walked to his desk
and sat down behind it.

What god with a bad sense of humor had brought the
woman to Venezuela and then deposited her outside this
office on the one day in weeks—in *weeks*, dammit!—he
had chosen to stop by?

It was insane.

"Insane," Antonio muttered, slapping his palms
against his desk.

How could he have had the misfortune of coming
across her again? Hadn't once been enough? His behavior that night in Denver had tormented him for days
afterward. The knowledge that he'd wanted a woman
like that—a woman who represented everything he most
despised—as if he were some sexually starved
adolescent . . .

His mouth twisted. The empty-headed blonde he'd
been with that night had ended up a very happy woman.

"Oh, Antonio," she'd kept saying in a little-girl voice
that made his teeth rattle, but not even burying himself
in her time and time again had been enough to erase the
anger blazing inside him, the ugly knowledge that he'd
made a fool of himself over a woman like the haughty
American.

He, of all men, knew what women of her class were
like. They were all the same, no matter what their
nationality: overbred, self-centered, amoral seekers of
pleasure who were contemptuous of anyone without
blood as blue as theirs. . . .

There was a tap at the door. Antonio looked up, his
face set in grim lines.

"Come in," he snapped.

The door swung open, and she stepped into the room.

She was pale; her face was shiny and devoid of
makeup. Her rain-soaked hair was slicked back behind

her ears, giving her a look that was, he knew, deceptively vulnerable. Her tussle with her would-be assailant had left her with a rip in her T-shirt, and her sandals—which he assumed were supposed to be white—were wet and gray from their dousing in the sudden cloudburst.

She looked like a half-drowned rat, Antonio thought with some satisfaction—except it wasn't really true. Bedraggled or not, she held herself very straight and tall. And she was still beautiful, he thought suddenly, as beautiful as he had remembered.

Not that he gave a damn.

"*Señor.*"

Kyra cleared her throat. She'd done a lot of thinking in the past minutes, enough to decide that she just might have behaved less than politely. It was even possible—just barely so—that she might have behaved rather badly....

But just look at him sitting there, not even pretending politeness.

No. That wasn't the way to think. If she did, she wouldn't be able to deliver the little speech she'd prepared.

Never mind his insolence. His flaws were his business, not hers. Never mind that he'd kissed her, either. The kiss had been nothing but a show of male contempt, primitive but effective. From his point of view, of course, not hers. There had been that one split second when she'd felt as if she were caught in a dizzying spiral, as if—as if...

Kyra straightened her shoulders. What was done was done. Besides, what could you expect from a man who wore his machismo like a badge of honor?

The bottom line was that, like it or not, he had rescued her from what had been a most unpleasant situation. She'd begun by owing him a thank-you; now, she owed

him an apology, too. And even if she choked on the
words, they had to be said.

Kyra cleared her throat and began again. "*Señor*,"
she said, "I, ah, I think..."

"Shut the door, please."

Her eyes narrowed slightly at his tone but she did as
he'd asked.

"I think I owe you an apology," she said, this time
even managing what she hoped was a smile.

"Indeed," he said coldly.

All right, so he was going to extract his pound of flesh.
Well, let him. She would do the right thing anyway.

"Yes," she said. "You risked your neck for me,
and—"

"Believe me, *señorita*, there was never any danger to
my neck."

Damn the man anyway. How could he sound so in-
furiatingly smug?

"Nevertheless," Kyra said calmly, "I should have
thanked you. And—"

"You did. As I recall, you were effusive with your
thanks—until you realized who I was."

"Yes. Well, perhaps I—"

"How unkind fate can be, *señorita*, to think that you
should find yourself beholden to me, of all people."

"Look, I'm trying to be polite. You did me a favor
and—"

"A favor?" His lips drew back from his teeth. "You
will forgive me if I am blunt, but I believe the appropriate phrase is that I saved your ass!"

Color flew into Kyra's cheeks. "Well, what would you
like me to do about it? Grovel? Let me assure you, mister,
if that's what you're waiting for, you're going to have
to wait until hell freezes over!"

They glared at each other for a moment and then
Antonio rose to his feet.

"You have spirit, *señorita*. I have to admit that."

"Why not admit that you'll also accept my apology?" She marched toward him, her hand outstretched, determined to get it over with. "My name is Kyra Landon, and I'm grateful for what you did."

He looked at her hand just long enough for her to wonder if he was going to disregard it, and then he took it in his. For an instant, she wondered if he was going to raise her hand to his lips. Her heart did a racing dance in anticipation of feeling his mouth against her skin—but he only shook her hand before letting it go.

"I am Antonio Rodrigo Cordoba del Rey," he said stiffly. "I assure you, I only did what any man of honor would have done in the same situation. As for gratitude—it was Consuelo who heard the fuss outside and decided you were in need of assistance."

"Yes, she told me. I've already tha—"

"What on earth were you doing in La Guaira, señorita?" Antonio leaned back against his desk while a smile, as phony as a counterfeit bill, curled over his mouth. "Did you think it would be amusing to take a walk on the wild side?"

Kyra's head came up. "You've already asked me that," she said coldly. "And I've answered it."

"Well, whatever your reason for venturing into this area alone, I would advise you that in the future—"

"I don't need your advice, *señor*."

Antonio sat down behind his desk, tilted back his chair, and folded his arms over his chest. It was a posture as patronizing as it was infuriating—and so was the smile he gave her.

"You certainly need someone's."

Kyra's eyes flashed. "For God's sake! I should have known having a civil conversation with you would be impossible!"

"On the contrary, Miss Landon. If we were not having a civil conversation, I would tell you that you behaved like a fool today and almost paid the price for it."

"That's it! Goodbye, Mr. del Rey. I've no intention of standing here while you—"

"You Americans never fail to amuse me, *señorita*. You would not think of strolling the streets of your own cities without knowing where you were going, yet you pretend the rest of the world is a playground where you can do as you wish and never have to pay the consequences."

Kyra's spine stiffened. His tone was as condescending as his manner, and it hadn't escaped her notice that he'd not asked her to sit down.

Did he expect she would stand here like a child called to the principal's office, while *he* lectured *her* on her manners?

She smiled. "You're right, of course," she said pleasantly. "Unfortunately, I gave up reading *National Geographic* years ago. Otherwise, I'd have remembered how primitive your continent can be."

It was a lie, of course. All she'd seen of South America was Caracas, and it was as modern a city as any. But the taunt had struck home. Señor Antonio Rodrigo Whatever del Rey looked as if he'd like nothing so much as to slug her, which meant she'd finally managed to get in under that handsome hide of his.

The realization brought joy to her heart.

"Thank you so much for that sincere apology, Señorita Landon," he said sarcastically as he reached for the phone. "Now, if you will tell me the name of your hotel, I will call a taxi for you and send you back where you belong."

Back where she belonged . . . Kyra's smile faded. She'd almost forgotten.

Damn, she thought, oh, damn.

"Actually—actually, I'm not staying at a hotel."

"The address of your friends, then. What is it?"

Kyra looked at his hand, hovering over the telephone. Now was the time to tell him the truth, that she had no money, no credit cards, no passport....

Tell him that the only person she knew on this entire continent was him? No. Uh-uh. Not if she had to sleep in the street!

"I see no need to give you the address, Señor del Rey. I'm perfectly capable of telling it to the taxi driver myself."

Antonio smiled, though it made every muscle in his face ache. What was this Landon woman afraid of? Did she really think he would follow on her heels like a dog after a bitch in heat?

"As you wish," he said. "But you needn't worry, Miss Landon. The only interest I'd have in knowing where you are staying is so that I can be sure to avoid that part of the city."

"What an excellent idea."

Giving up any pretense at civility, he snatched up the phone. "Consuelo? Please call a taxi for our guest. No, you may not tell the cab company where she wishes to be taken. Miss Landon is saving that information for the fortunate driver whose job it will be to take her back to Caracas. Yes. Thank you, Consuelo."

He frowned, drew some papers toward him, and picked up a pen. After a moment, he looked up and made a show of arching his brows in surprise.

"Are you still here, Miss Landon?"

It pleased him to see a flush rise in her pale cheeks. "I apologize," she said coldly. "I hadn't realized I'd been dismissed."

Kyra pivoted on her heel and walked to the door, slamming it after her hard enough so the pictures on the walls rattled.

She *was* a brat, in every sense of the word! Antonio tossed the pen aside, pushed the papers away, and glared at the closed door.

He'd been right that night at the Arts Center when he'd decided that what Kyra Landon needed was to be brought to heel by a man.

But not by him. Hell, no. The job would be more trouble than it would be worth.

Suddenly, he was overwhelmed by the memory of how it had felt to hold her in his arms and kiss her. Her mouth had been as soft and sweet as the petals of a rose....

Antonio cursed under his breath. He dragged the stack of papers toward him and bent over them. After a while, he even calmed down enough so that what he was reading began to make sense.

Kyra let the taxi take her several blocks before she cleared her throat, leaned forward, and told the driver that she hadn't any money.

The cabbie stepped on the brakes and pulled to the curb.

"But I'm not really broke," she said quickly.

She started to explain everything: she'd been robbed, she'd missed her ship, she needed to report the theft to the police and to seek help at the American Embassy....

The driver managed to reduce it all to one simple essential.

"Have you money to pay me for this ride, *señorita*?"

Kyra hesitated. "Well, no," she said finally, "not right now. But tomorrow..."

"I am interested in today, not tomorrow."

Nothing she could say would change his mind. A couple of minutes later, she was standing in the road, watching the taillights of the taxi fade into the gathering darkness.

Try as she might, she couldn't help a little shudder of distress. The rain had stopped, but the promise of more hung heavily in the air. The road was desolate, and night was coming on quickly.

She needed help. That was obvious. But she hadn't the vaguest idea where to find it.

The sound of raucous male voices floated toward her. Kyra swung around. A trio of drunks was moving up the center of the road, shouting and laughing as they passed a whiskey bottle back and forth.

Kyra's heartbeat stumbled. She stepped back quickly, flattening herself into the doorway of a building, and held her breath until the men had staggered past. She waited until the night was once again shrouded in silence and then she edged out of the doorway and started walking.

Any place had to be better than staying here.

The rain had started again and she quickened her pace. The street was still deserted. That was good. But if a car came along...

Would that be any better? Wouldn't it be stupid to be any more trustful of somebody driving a car than of somebody walking?

Still, the first time a pair of yellow headlights pierced the gloom, she stepped out into the road, waving her arms.

The car swept by her without even slowing down.

Kyra took a deep breath and continued walking.

The next time she heard a car approaching, she ran farther into the road.

"Hey," she yelled.

Water splattered her skirt as an ancient pickup truck wheezed past.

Kyra stood staring after it, and then she began trudging along again. All right, then. She'd just keep walking. Maybe she'd get lucky. Maybe a police car would come along, or another taxi. She wouldn't be stupid this time; she'd wait until they got to Caracas before she told the driver she had no—

Something, or someone, hissed at her from the darkness and a dark shape skittered past her toes. As it did, she heard the throaty roar of an engine. Without hesitating, Kyra raced into the middle of the road and jumped up and down.

"Stop," she yelled.

Tires squealed against wet asphalt as the headlights picked her out. She danced back as the vehicle swerved, shot past her, spun crazily and finally came to a stop.

She stared at the car. It was low and long—a Jaguar, perhaps. Not that it mattered. What did matter was the sinking feeling in the pit of her stomach as the driver's door opened.

No, she thought, please, no. Not again...

"Mother of us all," Antonio snarled. He stormed toward her and clamped his hands on her shoulders. "What are you trying to do to me?"

Kyra's chin tilted up a notch. "I had no idea it was you. In fact, had I known—"

"Am I fated for disaster at your hands?"

"Disaster at *my* hands?" Kyra tossed her wet hair from her eyes and glared at him. "I was not the one going a hundred miles an hour on a wet road, was I?"

"What are you doing here? Are you trying to kill me? Or will you be satisfied simply to drive me insane?"

"Isn't it amazing?" Kyra wrenched free of his hands and folded her arms. "Men always think of themselves first!"

Antonio felt his fingers twitch. No court on earth would convict him, he thought grimly, and jammed his hands into his pockets.

"I don't understand," he said. "You were in a taxi. You should have been out of this area—out of my life—by now!"

Kyra shrugged. "I suppose."

"You suppose?" His jaw tightened. "What does that mean, you 'suppose'?"

She stared back at him. "It means," she said, "that I need a ride into Caracas."

"You need a ride into..." Antonio took a deep breath. "What happened to your taxi?" He looked around as if it might be hiding in the shadows. "Did it break down?"

"It left."

"Left? What do you mean, left? Taxis don't leave, for God's sake!"

Kyra hesitated, but what was the point? It was night, it was raining, and she was too desperate to go on pretending. "They do when you haven't any money to pay for them."

Antonio cocked his head. "What are you talking about, woman?"

"My money was stolen," she said bluntly, "I haven't got a single bolivar."

"You mean, the cabdriver...?"

"A man on a motorbike snatched my purse."

"I don't understand. When did this happen? Surely not before that fiasco outside my office?"

Kyra sighed. "Look, I'll answer all your questions—"

"You most certainly will!"

"But could we please continue this discussion inside your car?"

Please? Had Kyra Landon really said "please"? For the first time, Antonio took a good look at the creature standing before him.

If she'd looked like a half-drowned rat a while ago, then there were no words to describe her now. Her hair was plastered to her skull, water dripped from her chin and nose, and her skirt was splattered with mud.

It was a sight that should have brought a smile of satisfaction to his lips. Instead, he had to fight back the sudden, unreasoning desire to gather her into his arms and tell her that everything would be all right....

Hell, he thought. What insanity was this? He'd sooner comfort a piranha than this woman!

Irritably, Antonio wrenched open the door to the car.

"Well?" he demanded. "Are you going to get in and ruin the leather or are you hoping I'll toss you a life jacket?"

Kyra stiffened. For just a moment, she'd almost thought she'd glimpsed a speck of human kindness in Antonio del Rey, which only showed how muddled you could get after a long, wretched day.

"Spoken like a true gentleman," she said sweetly, and she flounced past him into the Jaguar.

CHAPTER FOUR

ACTUALLY, dripping all over the Jaguar's leather seats sounded like a pretty good idea, but it turned out to be impossible. She'd hardly settled into the seat when Antonio reached into his breast pocket and pulled out a white handkerchief.

"Here," he said brusquely, tossing it into her lap. "Dry yourself off."

By the time she finished blotting the rain from her face, the handkerchief was soaked. What was protocol in this kind of situation? Did she hand this wet bit of linen back, or did she hang on to it? After a moment, she sighed, balled it into her fist, and sat back.

"Put your seat belt on."

Her head swung toward Antonio. Dry your face, put on your seat belt...

"Certainly," she said. "Anything else you'd like me to do?"

"Yes," he said coldly. "Tell me where in Caracas I am to take you."

Nowhere. There was nowhere to take her, not in this entire country. She had no money, no passport, no friends. She knew no one on this continent, in fact, except the stern-faced dictator seated beside her.

The thought sent a chill up her spine, and she gave a quick, inadvertent shudder.

"Are you cold?"

Kyra blinked. "What?"

Antonio shot her an impatient glance. "I thought I saw you shudder a moment ago."

"Did I?" She forced a smile to her lips. "I hadn't realized..."

"There is a jacket behind you. Put it on."

"That's not necessary."

"*Por Dios*, must everything be an argument?" He took one hand from the wheel, reached behind him, and snatched up the jacket. "Put it on, please," he snapped, dropping the garment in her lap.

Please? Who was he kidding? His tone made it clear that she had no real choice in the matter. Kyra's mouth turned down as she slipped the jacket around her. It was soft and warm, and it smelled faintly—and pleasantly—of its owner.

Kyra frowned and sat up straighter.

"Your wish is my command, sir," she said briskly.

If she'd meant to insult him, she hadn't succeeded. He laughed and looked across at her.

"Keep thinking that way," he said, "and we'll get along very well."

Kyra looked at him. "Has anyone ever told you you're living in another century?"

A smile curved across his lips. "Ah," he said softly, "a feminist."

"Only you would think so."

Antonio sighed. "You will be rid of me soon enough," he said. "Where am I to drop you off in Caracas?"

Kyra shifted uneasily in her seat. Now was the time to tell him she wasn't visiting friends as she'd let him believe, that the *Empress* had sailed without her.

But what then? Where could she ask him to take her? The thought of having to tell him that she didn't know where to go or what to do was too embarrassing.

"Well?"

She shrugged her shoulders. "It's—it's not far now," she said. "I'll tell you where when we get there."

What would she say when they got into the heart of the city? Where could she ask him to let her off? More to the point, how had she gotten into such an awful mess? The Jaguar raced through the night as her brain proposed and discarded a hundred different ideas.

She'd set off on an adventure meant to turn her life in a new direction; instead, she was broke, reduced to taking commands from a South American dictator—or had she been right in the first place? Was he Spanish? It was impossible to tell from his name, that long, rolling mouthful of poetic syllables. It was impossible to tell from his looks, either. That thick, inky black hair, the chiseled features, the golden-toned skin might have been Old World or New.

But those eyes, those shockingly blue eyes. What were they? Gorgeous, that was for certain. He might have the heart and soul of a penny-ante tyrant but...

"I am still waiting, Kyra."

She looked at him. "For what?"

"For an explanation of why you let me put you into a cab without admitting you could not pay for it."

"I, ah, I..."

"You what?"

I didn't want to owe you anything else, she thought, but she didn't say it. If she didn't come up with something clever soon, she was going to be in his debt again, she was going to have to ask him to lend her at least enough money to pay for a meal and a hotel room....

"Did you think the cabbie would take you into Caracas out of the goodness of his heart?"

"No, not exactly, but..."

Antonio's hands tightened on the wheel. She was typical of her class, he thought furiously. She knew nothing of the real world. As far as she was concerned, life was all sweet privilege.

"It was stupid, refusing to tell me you had no money," he said sharply.

Kyra swung toward him, her eyes flashing. "You know, you might want to consider that there might be extenuating circumstances before you call someone stupid. It's not always a good idea to try jamming your opinion down someone's throat!"

"Had you told me the truth," he said coolly, "I would have paid for your taxi."

"That was the last thing I wanted."

A disdainful smile curled over his mouth.

"I see," he said. "You would rather take your chances with the night than ask me for help, is that right?"

"I just didn't see that my problem was any of your concern."

"An admirable attitude," he said, his voice sharp with sarcasm. "Yet it seems to have become my concern nonetheless."

She bit her lip and suffered the rebuke in silence. He was right—and unless she could think of something, she was going to have to eat an even larger dose of humble pie.

"I assume you reported the theft to the police?"

"No. And don't bother launching into another lecture, okay? There just wasn't time. I had to choose between finding a police station and trying to make it to my ship before it sailed, and—"

"Your ship?"

Kyra slid down a bit in the seat. The cat was out of the bag now.

"Yes," she muttered. "The *Empress of the Caribbean*. I was on a cruise, and this was one of the stops. And—"

"You said you were staying with friends."

"I didn't say that at all," she said smugly. "*You* said it. I just didn't correct you."

"I cannot believe this! One, you have no money. Two, you have no papers. Three—"

"Three, you're managing to make this sound like—like some kind of international incident! Look, it was a screwup, that's all. I'm sure I'm not the first passenger ever to get to the dock late. I just never dreamed the ship would sail without me. I mean, honestly, you would think the captain would—"

"I know precisely what you would think." Antonio's voice was chill. "That the captain would delay the sailing, that he would inconvenience everyone else for your comfort."

"No! I simply meant—"

"What were you doing, that you lost track of time?"

"I was shopping. And for your information—"

"Shopping." His lip curled. "Of course. The sport of the rich."

A gust of laughter burst from Kyra's lips. The sport of the rich? Was that what she'd been indulging in when she'd bought the T-shirts with the funny sayings and the straw bag shaped like a donkey?

"I am pleased that I am such a source of amusement to you," Antonio said grimly.

"It isn't that. It's just that you're wrong about what I was doing. The shopping, I mean. I was—"

She broke off in midsentence. What was she doing, explaining herself to this man? He wasn't just a dictator, he was a hypocrite! The sport of the rich indeed. What about him, with his fancy car and his custom-made clothes?

"Well? I am waiting to hear your explanation."

Kyra smiled thinly. "You'll have a long wait, then. Yes, I was shopping, and yes, it was fun. And you're right, I did, indeed, expect the captain to wait for me. Have I left anything out?"

"Yes." His voice was hard and cold. "You have left out where it is you wish to get out of my car. Perhaps you haven't noticed, but we have reached Caracas."

"You're right," she said icily. "I hadn't noticed. I was too busy thinking how much I dislike you, Señor del Rey, and what a great pleasure it will be to get out of this car!"

"For the last time, woman, where shall I let you off?"

Kyra glared out the window. The streets were crowded with pedestrians, there were bright street lamps everywhere, but best of all, there was a big hotel just ahead.

"Here," she snapped.

Antonio swerved toward the curb, ignoring the sudden blare of horns from the cars he'd cut off.

"My pleasure," he said.

The car had barely rolled to a stop when Kyra flung the door open. She undid her belt, flung off his jacket, and tossed it into his lap.

"Goodbye, Señor del Rey," she said as she stepped out of the car. "Thank you for a memorable day."

"The same to you, Miss Landon."

The door slammed shut. The gears shrieked in protest as Antonio jammed through them and swung out into traffic.

What an impossible woman! Such insolence. Such icy coldness. Such a certainty that the world was hers....

And such legs. Was it really necessary to have sat like that, with her legs stretched out and crossed at the ankle? Her perfume had annoyed him, too. Why hadn't the rain drowned its soft, haunting fragrance? And her hair. If she had only bothered to keep the comb Consuelo had lent her, she might not have had to let it dry that way, tousled around her face so that he could only think that this must be the way she would look rising from his bed after a long, sweet night in his arms.

Thank the gods, he had seen the last of her.

Antonio stepped down hard on the gas pedal and drove off.

Half a dozen blocks away, he stood on his brakes, setting off another barrage of horn blasts as he swung to the curb again.

Did Kyra Landon have a functional brain in her head? For that matter, did he?

Antonio pounded the heel of his hand against the steering wheel.

No money. No credit cards. How would she pay for a hotel room? Without a passport or visa, how would she prove she had not entered the country illegally? This wasn't the United States, dammit; things were not always so simple here.

Hell, he thought, what did it matter? She disliked him, he disliked her. And, as she had said, the problem was hers, not his. She could try explaining herself to the hotel manager, perhaps even to the police.

The police, he thought, drumming his fingers against the steering wheel. If they got involved, she might very well end up spending the night in jail. She might even spend the weekend there, unless she could convince someone to phone the American Embassy. Even if she did, who knew what the embassy could, or would, do?

Well, so what? A couple of nights behind bars might do a woman like that some good. He had spent a night in jail once, years ago when he and half a dozen other losers had been yanked out of a waterfront bar in some backwater town; he could still remember how quickly eight hours on a stained mattress in a roach-infested cell had changed his mind about laughing at the law....

"Dammit," Antonio said fiercely.

He jammed the car into gear, shot out from the curb, and did a kamikaze U-turn straight across the lanes of oncoming traffic.

* * *

His timing couldn't have been better. She was coming out the main entrance of the hotel just as he reached the corner. Her head was up, her shoulders were back, but something in her pallor told him that things had not gone well.

The doorman gave her a sharp look as she marched past. Her pace quickened. Suddenly, a man came hurrying out the door. He said something to the doorman, who frowned and took a step after Kyra.

"*Señorita*," he shouted.

She didn't look back.

Antonio cursed under his breath, reached across to the passenger door and flung it open. Then he pounded his fist against the horn.

"Kyra!" he yelled.

She hesitated and looked toward the road. He shouted her name again and saw her face light up and her lips mouth his name.

"Get in," he barked as she raced to the car. Once she had, he revved the engine and they flew away from the curb.

"Oh, Antonio," she said breathlessly, "you came along just in time!"

He looked over at her. Her eyes were shining with excitement. He wanted to do something, but what? Grab her and shake her until her teeth rattled? Kiss her until her mouth opened to his?

"Are they following us?" she said, peering over her shoulder. She gave a little laugh as she swung toward him again. "You should have seen what happened in there, Antonio. It was like a spy movie. I asked for a room, and—"

"What in hell is the matter with you?" he snarled. "Do you think this is all a game?"

"Of course not. I'm just trying to tell you what—"

"Did you think they would show you to a suite and tell you that you could pay for it in the next millennium?"

Her smile was quickly fading. "Stop yelling at me! And stop looking as if—as if I need a keeper!"

"That is precisely what you do need," Antonio said furiously.

Kyra glared back at him. Moments ago, when she'd seen his car and heard his voice calling her, her heart had lifted with joy. What had been a terrifying experience had suddenly become an adventure once she knew Antonio was there to protect her....

To protect her? She didn't want that! What on earth had made her think something so stupid? Come to think of it, what had made her think she was happy to see Antonio del Rey again?

"All right," she said coldly, "you've had your fun."

"Fun? Is that what this is? I thought it was aiding and abetting a criminal."

Kyra flushed. "I am not a criminal," she said stiffly.

"You ran away from the manager of the hotel."

"Did you expect me to wait while he called the police?"

"Why not?" Antonio said, his eyes on the road. "You could have reported the theft of your things."

"Yes, but—but I had the feeling the police might not have believed me any more than the manager did."

"What did you tell him?"

"The truth. That I'd been a passenger on a ship, that a thief snatched my pocketbook—"

"What he saw," Antonio said coldly, "is a woman who looks as if she'd slept in her clothes."

Kyra flushed. Her hand went to her hair in a defensive gesture.

"I know I'm a mess, but..."

She wasn't a mess. She was disheveled-looking, yes, but she was still beautiful. More beautiful than the first time he'd seen her. She looked like a real woman now, not some designer's mannequin.

Antonio frowned. What did he care how she looked? His problem now was what to do with her.

"Anyway," she said, her tone frigid, "you didn't have to aid and abet me, if you think I'm lying."

He sighed. "I never said you were lying. What I said was—"

"I know what you said. Do me a favor and don't go through that again." She looked at him. "Why'd you come back anyway?"

"Because it occurred to me that precisely what did happen might happen."

She hesitated. "I suppose I should thank you...."

"I have seen you in action, Kyra. I would not willingly inflict you on anyone, even the police."

It was a moment for a clever response, but suddenly she was fresh out. She was tired, she was hungry, and she was feeling more and more desperate.

"Let's make a deal," she said wearily. "I won't snipe at you if you won't snipe at me, okay?"

Antonio started to respond, then thought better of it. She must be exhausted, he decided, and with a shrug, he gave in.

"All right," he said, "I agree."

They drove in silence for a few minutes and then she sighed.

"I should go to the embassy...." To her horror, she heard a sudden tremor in her voice. She cleared her throat and started over. "I have to do something."

Antonio lifted his eyebrows. "Are you asking my advice?"

She hesitated. "I'm open to ideas," she admitted.

And, just that readily, it came to him. It probably would have sooner if the woman hadn't gotten him so angry.

He could solve her problem with just a couple of phone calls. He knew at least half a dozen officials, American and Venezuelan, who would be happy to win his favor. He smiled, thinking of how they'd fall all over themselves in their eagerness to please him by helping someone he vouched for. He could make things right in no time.

"Why are you smiling?"

Antonio looked at her. "I've thought of a way to help you."

"Have you really?" She smiled, too. "Tell me."

He shook his head. "First, we'll have dinner. And then I will explain."

"Dinner! But—"

He pulled to the curb and shut off the ignition. "Dinner first," he said sternly.

Actually, he thought as he stepped from the car, there was no reason not to tell her about his plan now but there were a few last details to think through; he wanted to be certain there were no kinks before he explained it.

"Antonio, I don't want dinner first! I want to know—"

Kyra gritted her teeth. He wasn't listening, not that that was anything new. He'd already shut his door and now he was opening hers.

"Come," he said in that imperious tone she'd come to hate.

"Dammit, Antonio—"

"Is it impossible for you to do as you're told?" He could feel his good mood fading as she went on sitting there, glaring at him. Finally he muttered something, bent down, undid her seat belt, and drew her on to the sidewalk.

"Where are you taking me?" she demanded.

"To a restaurant," he said as he clasped her elbow and hustled her along beside him. "It is late, and I am tired and hungry. I want a meal and some wine, and then we will talk."

"You might have asked what *I* wanted!"

Antonio swung toward her. "Very well," he said curtly. "I am asking you now. Do you wish to join me for dinner, or would you prefer to sit in the car and sulk?"

She glared at him. Was he trying to make her feel like a fool?

"Make up your mind quickly, *querida*. I told you, I am hungry."

"Don't call me that! I don't like it."

"And I don't like women who argue about everything." His hand closed on her arm again and he all but dragged her into the recesses of what was obviously an expensive restaurant.

A fawning headwaiter led them to a booth. Kyra's temper smoldered like a lit fuse. She flounced into her seat, opened her menu, and buried her nose in it.

The audacity of the man! Did he go through life bullying everyone, or was it women who brought out the dictator in him?

"...prefer, Kyra?"

She looked up from the menu. "Pardon me?" she said, her tone frigid.

"I asked if you preferred a Burgundy or a Pinot Noir."

"How nice that you should condescend to ask." She snapped the menu shut and put it down. "I don't want wine at all."

Antonio decided to ignore the display of temper. She had to be as hungry and as out of sorts as he was, which would make her all the happier to hear his plan.

He closed his menu, too, and looked at the waiter. "We will have red, Carlos, a Chateauneuf-Du-Pape, the same as I had last time, *si*? And steaks. And—"

"Didn't you hear me? I don't want wine. And I don't want steak. I'd rather have—"

"It is the specialty here, Kyra." He smiled. "The only question is, do you wish your steak rare or well-done?"

Color swept into her cheeks. The waiter was taking in every bit of this routine with a faint but contemptuous smile. Were all men members of the same universal club?

Kyra leaned forward. "Listen here, Antonio. For the last time, I don't want—"

"Rare, then, Carlos. And baked potatoes and green salads, *si*?"

Antonio sat back as the waiter hurried off. "You will feel better after you have eaten, Kyra, and then I shall offer you the solution to your problem."

How she despised his handsome face! *He* would come up with a solution to her problem? Well, why not? He had dragged her in here, he had ordered her meal...hell, he was taking over her life! Well, she'd put a stop to that!

"Carlos," she called.

The waiter was halfway across the room, but Kyra's voice carried. He turned—actually, half the diners nearby turned, but she was beyond caring—and came scurrying back. He paused beside the table and looked at Antonio.

"*Señor*? Is there a problem?"

"The *señor* didn't call you," Kyra said coldly. "I did. And yes, there is a problem. I don't like being ignored."

Antonio's eyes narrowed. He watched in silence as Kyra ordered Carlos to bring her broiled fish, sliced tomatoes, and a glass of iced tea. Her tone was sharp and imperious.

It was an unpleasant performance for him to watch and for the hapless waiter to endure, but it was illuminating. This, after all, was the real Kyra Landon.

Antonio's mouth thinned. He remembered what he had thought this afternoon, that she needed a man to bring her to heel. He recalled what he had thought only a little while ago, that a night in the purgatory of a jail might do the same thing.

Perhaps he had been right on both counts, he thought coldly. And in that instant, with a dark thrill of anticipation, he knew exactly what offer he would make her.

The waiter shot Antonio a questioning glance when Kyra finally fell silent. Antonio nodded.

"That's all right, Carlos," he said quietly. "Do as the *señorita* says."

Kyra's heart was thudding. She'd never behaved so badly in her life, but it had been worth it just to see the look on Antonio's face.

"I have changed my mind," he said. "I have decided to tell you my plan now, instead of waiting until we finish eating."

Kyra smiled. Her show of independence had had the desired effect after all.

"Yes?" she said. "What is it?"

A muscle knotted in Antonio's cheek. "I own an island off the coast. It's called San Sebastian. When I am in this part of the world, it is where I live. It is where I was headed this evening before you leaped out into the road."

"I'm sure that's very interesting," she said impatiently, "but what has it to do with me?"

His smile was slow and dangerous enough to make her breath catch.

"You will live on my island for a week, Kyra. At the end of that time, I will—"

Kyra's temper ignited like a fireworks display on the Fourth of July. She rose from the table so swiftly that her chair fell back and clattered to the floor. The restaurant went silent; every eye turned to her again but she didn't care.

"I'd sooner live in the street!"

Antonio laughed. "How about a cell?" he said, his voice silken. "Does that have equal appeal?"

Kyra tossed her napkin on the table. Head high, she marched through the room and out the door.

He took his time pushing back his chair and getting to his feet, waving off Carlos as he came hurrying forward.

"It's quite all right," he said, and tossed a fat wad of bills on the table.

He saw her as soon as he stepped outside, walking swiftly along the road. He got in the car and set out after her. When he drew alongside, he put the transmission in neutral and stepped out.

Kyra swung around as soon as he touched her shoulder, her hands flailing in fury.

"Get away from me!"

Antonio laughed softly. He put his arms around her, drew her slowly to him despite the ferocity of her struggles.

"If you don't let me go, I'll scream!"

"Scream, Kyra. Perhaps the *policía* will come." He bent his head until his mouth was a whisper from hers. "And then you can choose between their hospitality and mine."

"I'll kill you for this, Antonio, so help me...I'll—"

His mouth came down on hers, hard and hot and hungry. She beat her fists against his chest, sank her teeth into his lip, but nothing could stop him. He kept kissing her, his lips moving on hers, his tongue stroking across the seam of her mouth, until, with a little sob, she did what he wanted, what she wanted, and opened her mouth to him.

Antonio drew her tightly against him. Kyra felt her breasts flatten against his chest, felt the race of his heart against hers. His hands slipped to her bottom; he lifted her up toward him so that his erection pressed hard against the cradle of her femininity...

And then he let go of her.

Her eyes flew open; she stared at him and felt as if she were awakening from the deepest of dreams.

"You see, *querida*," he said calmly, "if I wanted you, I would have you." He folded his arms, his expression impassive. "But I do not want you."

He saw the confusion and the vulnerability flash across her face. For the space of a heartbeat he hesitated—but then he remembered who he was and who he had been, and his face hardened.

"Have you ever worked for your living?" He smiled tightly, his eyes on hers, and his voice became almost gentle. "Never mind," he said. "I am sure we both know the answer."

She stared at him. "What are you driving at, Antonio?"

"I will employ you for a week's time, at the end of which I will see to it that you have a passport and a visa so you may leave the country unhindered. And I will pay you enough to get you home in the fashion to which you are accustomed."

"Employ me?" she said, her eyes searching his in puzzlement. "Give me a job, you mean?"

"Exactly."

"But—but doing what?"

His lips drew back from his teeth. "A good question. After all, what could a woman such as you do that would be of benefit to anyone?" His shoulders lifted in a lazy shrug. "I have a housekeeper. I shall let Dolores determine your skills and put you to work accordingly."

Kyra said nothing for a moment and then she gave a nervous laugh.

"This is a joke, right?"

The smile faded from Antonio's face. "I have never been more serious," he said coldly. "Now, make up your mind. Do you go with me to San Sebastian, or do I take you to the police station and let you try to convince them of your situation?"

She stared at him while the seconds flew by, overwhelmed by how much she hated this man! She was burning with the desire to spit in that arrogant face, to claw out those deep blue eyes....

"Well? What is your decision?"

"I'll be your bloody servant for a week," she said, her voice shaking with anger, "but I promise, Antonio, I'll get even someday."

Head high, she swept past him and got into the car.

CHAPTER FIVE

THAT Antonio del Rey owned a small, sleek plane he flew himself came as no surprise to Kyra.

Sitting beside him in the cockpit of the Cessna as the lights of the mainland slipped away beneath them, she thought wearily that nothing would ever surprise her again.

How could it, after today?

Kyra glanced at the small digital clock that glowed on the instrument panel. Twelve hours had passed since she'd stepped happily out of her cabin on the *Empress of the Caribbean* and set off for what should have been a pleasant day of sight-seeing and shopping. Instead, she'd been robbed, assaulted, abandoned—and now she was being carried off to who-knew-where by a South American tyrant!

She was furious with Antonio but almost as furious with herself. How could she have given in to such out-and-out blackmail? Wasn't she the woman who was done with letting men tell her what to do?

Damn! She should have told him to drive her straight to the door of the nearest police station.

"I'd rather take my chances with them," she should have said, "than go anywhere with a macho ape like you!"

Surely she wasn't the first tourist to find herself in such a fix.

Kyra looked out the window. The lights of the mainland had slipped away beneath them. They were flying over water now; except for a thin crescent moon, they were wrapped in inky blackness.

A knot of fear suddenly lodged in her throat.

My God, she thought, *what am I doing?*

She turned toward Antonio, her heart pounding. She had to tell him she'd changed her mind, demand that he turn the Cessna around and take her back.

But she couldn't do that. All she had left was her pride, and she was determined to get out of this with that pride intact. She hadn't a clue as to why Antonio wanted to humiliate her but she'd be damned if she'd make it easy for him.

She had no idea how much time had passed before she felt the angle of the plane change. They were starting their descent.

Kyra's hands knotted together in her lap. Take deep breaths, she told herself. Think calm thoughts.

The Cessna's landing lights illuminated a narrow landing strip carved out of the trees. The wheels touched down lightly and the plane gradually rolled to a stop.

Antonio shut off the engine and the silence of the tropical night surrounded them.

"We have arrived," he said.

Kyra looked at him. Her heart was beating so quickly she was afraid it might burst through her chest but she met his gaze coolly.

"I'm glad you told me," she said. "I never would have guessed."

She could see his jaw tighten. "It is late, and I am sure you are as tired as I am. I suggest we dispense with any verbal games and go to the house."

The house? What house? She couldn't see anything out there but the darkness. Where were all the people? Where were the roads and the lights from cars speeding along them?

"If you have any questions that cannot wait until morning, ask them now."

She had a dozen questions, starting with wanting to know why he was doing this to her, but she'd sooner have choked than ask even one.

"What? No questions?"

"None."

"Good." He smiled tightly. "In that case, welcome to my island."

She stared after him as he opened the door and dropped lightly to the ground. A bubble of wild laughter rose in her throat. Welcome to his island? He had to be kidding. Welcome to my parlor, said the spider to the fly.

Wait a minute. What did he mean, *his* island? Surely San Sebastian couldn't be his alone. Surely he hadn't meant that.

"Kyra?"

She turned to the door just behind her. Antonio was standing on the ground, looking up at her. He held out his hand.

She nodded coolly, as if being dragged off to a dot of land thousands of miles from home were something that happened to people all the time. But her fingers were cold and stiff as she fumbled with her seat belt. At last the belt came undone, and she took a deep breath, determined not to let him see her fear.

"Give me your hand," he said, "and I will help you to the ground."

She looked down. The ground might have been two feet below her or two miles; between the darkness and the fear, she couldn't tell. But she'd have stepped off the Empire State Building without a parachute if the alternative meant accepting a favor from him.

"I can manage," she said coldly—but as she stepped from the plane, Antonio moved forward and caught her in his arms.

"Getting out of a plane is not the same as getting out of a limousine! Don't be an idiot, Kyra. It's dark, and..."

His throat seemed to close once she was in his arms. He had not intended to make anything personal of the contact; he had reached out to her instinctively once he realized that she'd forgotten she'd had to climb up in order to get into the plane, and yet the instant her hands fell to his shoulders, his body had seemed to become electrified.

He wanted to lower her to the ground quickly, to do away with the feel of her small hands, the warmth of her breath against his face. But he couldn't. It was like being caught in a dream where everything happens in slow motion: her breasts brushing lightly against his chest, her belly and thighs grazing his...

Dios, he thought, why had he brought her here? It was an incredibly stupid thing to have done. So what if she needed a lesson in humility? This was not a modern-dress version of *The Taming of the Shrew*, dammit. It was real life. It was his life, and he had better things to do with it than stand by while his head and his hormones fought it out.

And that was what had been happening to him since the night he'd first seen her.

Had he learned nothing over the years?

He had made this mistake before, so long ago that the memory was only a whisper. Then, he had been too young and too stupid to know that nothing would ever make his blood the proper shade of blue, that what happened in bed with an ice princess had nothing to do with what happened in the heart of a man who knew what it was to earn his living with his hands.

"Dammit, Antonio, will you put me down?"

Antonio blinked. She was not just struggling in his arms, she was shaking from having suffered his touch. He took a deep breath, set her on the ground, and lifted his hands from her with exaggerated care.

"Forgive me," he said sarcastically. "But you see, there is no doctor on San Sebastian. If you should hurt yourself, what use will you be to me?"

"How touching." Her chin came up. It was hard to sound cool and unconcerned when she was still trembling from being in his arms. Damn him! How could he make her feel that way? Kyra forced a scornful smile to her lips. "I wonder, Antonio, do you show all your servants that much concern?"

"Do not worry. I will see to it that there is clean straw in the dungeon, and since tomorrow is Saturday, I will supplement your ration of bread and water with scraps from the kitchen."

"What a charming sense of humor."

"Indeed," he said dryly. He took her arm, ignoring her attempt to wrench free, and guided her to a pickup truck that loomed ahead of them in the darkness.

He let her scramble into the cab herself. Then he turned the key and set off along a narrow road that led through the trees to the house.

He parked in the courtyard, just inside the old wrought-iron gate he'd found during his last trip to Spain and had shipped here. The house was dark but Dolores had left the outside lights on and he could see two of his dogs come charging from the gardens, their tails wagging with excitement as they danced around the truck.

"Are those mastiffs?"

He looked over at Kyra. "They are crossbreeds. But they will not hurt you unless—"

Kyra flung her door open and stepped down.

"Dammit, woman!"

Antonio jumped from the truck, but the huge dogs had already turned toward her.

"Hello there," she said softly.

The dogs regarded her in silence. One took a stiff-legged step forward. Kyra held out her hand.

"What beautiful babies you are," she murmured. "Come here and let me get a better look at you."

The dogs approached warily. Antonio knew there was no real danger—he had trained the animals himself and they would respond instantly to his command—but Kyra had no way of knowing that.

He frowned as he watched her. Workmen had been on the island just a few weeks ago—big, burly men with thickly muscled arms and shoulders—and none would come past the gate when the dogs were loose. And yet, here was this slender woman who had just gotten down on her knees and put her arms around the enormous necks of the animals.

"They're wonderful!"

Kyra was looking up at him, her arms still looped about the dogs' necks, her face creased in an enormous smile.

Antonio didn't smile back. "And you are a foolish woman. You did not even consider that the dogs might hurt you."

"Well, you said they wouldn't."

"You were out of the truck before I finished speaking."

"Well, I—I..." She smiled again, with a little less certainty but without letting go of the dogs. "I really didn't think about it. I've always loved dogs, and these guys are just so beautiful...."

Antonio frowned. He wanted to tell her that you could never judge a creature by its beauty. But there was something about the sight of her as she knelt between the dogs that made it difficult to maintain his anger.

"Handsome," he said after a moment. He smiled. "I think they would prefer you think of them as handsome rather than as beautiful." Kyra laughed. He watched as she stroked the big heads and then he cleared his throat. "So then," he said, "you have dogs of your own at home?"

"Oh no." She looked up at him, her smile dimming. "I always wanted a dog but—"

"But?"

"But, my father didn't approve. He said dogs were dirty creatures that served no useful function, and..." She shrugged her shoulders in a gesture Antonio instinctively knew was more telling than the words she'd spoken. "What are their names?"

He hesitated. He had taken a lot of ribbing about those names from anyone who heard them.

"Brutus? Thor? Zeus?"

Antonio couldn't help smiling. "Not quite. The big black one is called Vergonzoso."

Kyra laughed. "Bashful?"

"*Sí.* And the smaller one with the brindled coat is called—"

"Let me guess." The dog had collapsed on its back, all four legs waving in the air as it demanded to have its belly rubbed. "This one's name just has to be Bobo."

Antonio grinned. "Dopey. Yes. But how—"

"Oh, it was easy. I must have seen *Snow White and the Seven Dwarfs* a dozen times when I was little." She rose gracefully to her feet, the dogs close beside her. "I just wouldn't have expected—"

"I wanted to give them names that would forever separate them from their old lives." Antonio reached down and absently rubbed the two big heads that were butting against his legs. "And the names are appropriate." He smiled. "The black one would not come out from behind the furniture for the first month after I brought him home. The brindle insisted on behaving like a clown, even though the scars on his body were proof that someone had worked diligently at changing his disposition.''

Kyra's eyes widened. "You mean—"

"I found them when they were puppies, in an alley behind the hotel I was staying at in New York City." His mouth thinned. "It seems as if dog fighting has its aficionados everywhere."

"Thank God you rescued this pair," she said with a shudder.

"They had rescued themselves by running away," Antonio said with a little smile. "I simply adopted them."

"And turned them into sweethearts," Kyra said, smiling down at the animals.

"I did not turn them into anything but what Nature intended."

"Yes, I know. But people always say such unkind things about mastiffs—"

"They say even worse things about crossbreeds."

There was a bitterness in Antonio's voice that Kyra had not heard before. She looked at him.

"I never thought about it, but I suppose you're right."

His eyes turned cool. "I know I am right." A long moment passed and then he frowned and nodded toward the stone steps that led to the front door. "Come," he said brusquely. "It is very late, and I am sure you are exhausted."

What was the sense in denying it? Kyra nodded. Suddenly, she knew she was more than exhausted; she was tired enough so that she was light-headed.

"Yes, I am. I..."

She swayed unsteadily and reached out to the iron railing for support, but before she could grasp it, Antonio scooped her into his arms.

Kyra's face flooded with color. "Put me down!"

"I will," he said coolly, "when I am sure you will have a soft bed to fall on instead of stone steps."

Of course. She remembered his earlier admonition that there was no doctor here, and if she hurt herself, she would be useless. But somehow the knowledge that lifting her into his arms and holding her this way was just a convenience for his own peace of mind did nothing to keep her breath from quickening at how it felt to be so close to him.

"Put your arms around my neck, Kyra."

She hesitated, which only made her feel more foolish. His tone was brusque, as impersonal as the reason he'd lifted her in the first place.

Slowly, her eyes downcast, she looped her arms around him. Her fingers brushed the thick, dark hair that grew low on his collar; it felt like the softest silk and she fought against the swift desire to bury her fingers in it, to turn her face to his neck and touch her mouth to his tanned throat....

Dios, Antonio thought, what had he done to himself?

There was no need to be standing here with Kyra in his arms. She had suddenly gone pale with exhaustion; she'd reached out to the railing for support. All he'd had to do was take her arm and steady her.

Instead, he'd gathered her up in an embrace. It meant nothing, he'd told her. And now he was telling the same thing to himself.

But it was a lie.

He caught his breath as he felt the cool brush of her fingers against the nape of his neck. If only she would bury her hands in his hair, drag his head down to hers. He ached with self-loathing for wanting to possess her, but it didn't change his need.

He bent his head so that his chin just brushed her cap of dark, shining hair. It felt like silk and smelled of lemons and he thought how strange it was that something as mundane as the scent of citrus should suddenly make his heart beat faster.

"Kyra?"

His voice was a sigh in the silence of the night. Her face tilted up to his, her eyes wide and so pale in the glint of the moon that they might have been starlight.

"Kyra," he said again, and as her lashes drifted slowly to her cheeks, Antonio brought his mouth to hers.

Her mouth was satin. It was velvet. It was as soft as a flower and just as sweet. His arms tightened around her and he groaned softly as her hands did what he had dreamed they might, her fingers sweeping into his hair, her palms cupping the back of his head so that he might deepen the kiss.

He did, his tongue sweeping across her lips and into her mouth and now it was she who groaned with desire.

Antonio's hand moved to the side of her breast. His fingers brushed upward, kissing the nipple with flame, turning it hard beneath her cotton shirt.

He whispered something in Spanish against her mouth, turned her closer to him, exulting in the wild leap of her heart against his and the moans that slipped from her parted lips.

"Señor del Rey?"

Antonio lifted his head. Light from the open front door spilled out onto the steps, blinding him. He backed down quickly into the shadows, while he fought to recover his senses.

"Dolores?"

"*Sí, señor.*" His housekeeper, a small, stocky woman in a long flannel robe, peered cautiously into the night. "I thought I heard the dogs, but no one came to the door."

"Antonio," Kyra whispered, "put me down. Please."

"I apologize if I woke you, Dolores," he said, ignoring her.

"No, no, *señor*. I was reading when..." The housekeeper's eyes widened as Antonio stepped forward into the light. "Is that a woman?"

Antonio nodded. "It is."

Her eyes lifted to his. "Is she ill?"

"She is tired." He came up the steps and into the high-ceilinged foyer, his footsteps loud against the tiled floor. "She has had a long and very difficult day."

"Ah, I see," Dolores said wisely.

It was all Antonio could do not to smile for he knew she didn't see at all. He had never brought a woman here before. Not that he was bringing Kyra here in the way Dolores meant. Not that she was staying. Not that he was really going to force her to keep their unholy bargain.

"*Señor*?" Dolores hesitated. "Shall I prepare something for her to eat?"

"A good idea. Some soup, perhaps. And a sandwich."

"Of course. And shall I bring it to the guest room or—or will she be sleeping in—in—"

"Oh, for heaven's sake!" Kyra's voice was rough with impatience. "I am perfectly capable of speaking for myself. And I am not a—a sack that needs carrying, thank you very much!"

Antonio frowned. "The stairs are long and you are tired. I was only—"

"Yes." Kyra shoved her hands against his chest and glared at him. "I know. You've already told me. You're trying to keep me from tripping or slipping or doing some fool thing like breaking my neck so you don't have to deal with a medical emergency." Her mouth straightened into an angry, thin line. "Will you put me down?"

"Ah, *señor*, if you do not need me..."

"Go on," Antonio said, his voice clipped. "Make our guest something to eat. I will show her to her room."

"I am not a guest," Kyra said furiously. She banged her fist on Antonio's shoulder and raised her voice to a shout. "Where is that old crone? Why did she run away? Is she so accustomed to seeing you carry your victims into your lair that she thinks nothing of it when she sees a woman struggling in your unwanted embrace?"

She cried out as Antonio's arms tightened around her.

"You were not struggling a little while ago, *querida*." His voice was low and harsh, his face grim as he started up the wide staircase. "You were as soft and compliant as a rabbit, and if we had not been interrupted you would have let me take you there on the steps, with the moonlight on your naked body."

It was painfully close to the truth. Whatever had happened outside in the courtyard was beyond Kyra's comprehension. Antonio had touched her and suddenly she'd lost all connection to reality. That she hated him, that he had blackmailed her into coming here, that his contempt for her was matched only by her contempt for him, had become meaningless.

All that had mattered were his kisses. His touch. The feel of his strong, muscled arms around her, and the race of his heart against hers . . .

Antonio kicked open a door and stepped into a room dusted with moonlight. A huge, canopied bed stood on a raised platform in its center.

Kyra's struggles intensified. "Put me down, you—you tyrant!"

"Watch what you say to me, woman." His voice was icy as he shouldered the door closed behind him.

"You took advantage of me a few minutes ago. You know that you did! I wasn't myself. I—"

The breath whooshed from her lungs as Antonio dropped her in the center of the bed. She scrambled back against the pillows, her eyes flashing.

"I warn you, Antonio, if you touch me you're only going to make things worse. I'll—I'll go straight to the authorities on this island. I'll tell them you abducted me, I'll charge you with kidnapping. I'll— What's so funny?"

He was laughing at her, damn him, *laughing* at her, his hands on his hips and his dark head thrown back as if she had just cracked the funniest joke he'd ever heard.

Kyra reached for the first thing she could get her hands on, a small porcelain clock that stood ticking quietly on the beside table. She flung it at Antonio's head but he ducked as it hurtled past him and smashed into pieces against the wall.

"Damn you, what is so funny?"

"You, *querida*," he said, wiping his eyes. "Do you really think I am so desperate for a woman that I would force myself on such a sharp-tongued, skinny, bedraggled-looking creature as you?"

Color raced into her cheeks. "None of that seemed to be enough to stop you a little while ago!"

"As for your threats...you came to my island of your own volition."

"You blackmailed me into coming here!"

Antonio leaned back against the wall, his arms crossed.

"I offered you employment." A cool smile touched his lips. "I know the idea of exchanging work for money may be new to you but it is quite common, believe me."

"Go on, say whatever you like." Kyra glared at him. "When I file my complaint with the authorities—"

"Do you know how to fly a Cessna?" he asked politely. "Or were you planning on swimming to the mainland?"

"I'm talking about the authorities on this island. I'm sure you pay them all huge bribes to keep them in your pocket, but..." Her nostrils flared. "What's so amusing this time?"

"You are looking at the authority on this island, Kyra." He smiled. "There is no law here but the law I choose to impose."

"But—but what about the others who live here?"

"What others?" He laughed. "Surely you do not think that my housekeeper or the others who work for me dispute my decisions?"

She turned the color of sun-bleached linen. That was fine, Antonio thought grimly. She deserved a taste of fear. If this little episode in his life accomplished nothing else, it would be good to know that he had taught Kyra Landon she could not get away with such dangerous games, seeking a man's help only to condemn it when it was offered, teasing him with the promise of fire but turning to ice at his touch.

Not that he was blameless, he thought reluctantly. It had been stupid, letting his anger get the best of him so that he'd ended up bringing her here. As for the rest, she was everything he'd called her: sharp-tongued, bedraggled-looking, as impossibly stubborn and thick-skulled as the new Arabian stallion down in the stables behind the house.

Yet he couldn't seem to keep his hands off her.

Antonio turned and walked to the window. It was ridiculous. He'd been working long hours lately, what with flying back and forth between the States and South America while he tied up half a dozen deals that involved not just his shipping company but his real-estate holdings, too.

Was that why he was behaving with something less than his usual logic? Of course it was. The realization came as a relief.

All right, then. He had made a mistake. Tomorrow, he would rectify it. He would take her back to the mainland, set in motion the arrangements necessary to get her out of his life once and for all.

With a smile of relief, he turned and looked at her.

"I have reached a decision, Kyra."

"So have I!"

"Let me finish, please," he said calmly. "Tomorrow, I intend to—"

"I don't care what your intentions are, Antonio." Kyra's eyes flashed as she got to her feet. "I've changed my mind about our bargain. Take me back to Caracas."

She kept her eyes on his face and waited, her heart pounding. All the time he'd been standing here, brooding over her fate like some medieval tyrant, she'd been working up to this moment.

What she'd agreed to was stupid. Dealing with her brothers was one thing; giving in to the demands of Antonio Rodrigo Cordoba del Rey was quite another.

There was only one way to deal with men like him. You had to stand up to them and tell them what you wanted. If you didn't, they'd roll over you without a second thought.

"Well?" She looked at him, her cheeks flushed. "Did you hear me? I demand—"

"I told you once, Kyra." His voice was sharp. Who did she think she was? Who did she think *he* was, a boy to take her orders? "Watch how you speak to me."

"Why? Because you own this island?" Kyra flung out her arms. "Because you think you can force everybody to do your bidding?" She shot to her feet and stalked toward him. "You're so used to playing tin god that you can't imagine anyone standing up to you!"

Antonio fought to contain his temper, which was edging up toward the danger level.

"You try to blame your situation on me," he said coldly, "but you are in a mess of your own making. You have made foolish, even childish, decisions."

"Don't you dare lecture me!"

"I am simply saying—"

"I know what you're saying! That the world should shut up and salute when you give an order! Well, I'm not saluting. And I'm not staying here another minute!"

The last vestige of Antonio's control snapped. "I will not be spoken to like that by anyone, Kyra, least of all you!"

"And I will not take orders," Kyra said, her breathing rapid, "*especially* from a man like you!"

His hands whipped out and clasped her shoulders, hard.

"Be careful," he said between his teeth. "Be very careful of what you say."

"Let go of me, you—you bully!"

His hands bit into her flesh. "Kyra, I warn you—"

"Don't *you* warn *me*, you—you no-good bastard!"

Antonio flung her from him. "Dolores will awaken you in the morning," he said, his voice sharp as a razor, "and assign you your duties. I promise you, Kyra, you are going to spend a week on this island that you will never forget!"

The door slammed shut after him. Kyra stood absolutely still, fists clenched at her sides, and then she gave a little shriek of pure fury, flew to the door, and threw the lock.

"The same goes for you, Señor Dictator," she yelled.

She put her ear to the door, listening as Antonio's footsteps receded.

Then, at last, she let the tears come.

CHAPTER SIX

KYRA had no intention of waiting for the housekeeper to wake her the next morning.

She might have signed on to be Antonio's servant-of-the-week, she thought grimly as she sat up in bed, but she would not let him make her feel like a prisoner. She didn't need a wake-up call or a matron to escort her downstairs.

Her bedroom glowed with the soft, golden light of the Caribbean morning. It was, she had to admit, a handsome room, furnished in a dazzling pastiche of periods and styles that somehow came together with a breathtaking beauty.

Kyra walked to the window and looked out at the view. Her room overlooked a garden at the back of the house, which blazed with the lush colors of the tropics. Beyond, an emerald lawn stretched toward the azure sea visible in the distance.

A man was walking slowly through the gardens toward the house. Kyra stepped quickly back behind the curtains. It was Antonio; she knew it instantly, even though she had never seen him dressed so casually before. But even in denim cutoffs, a white T-shirt and tennis shoes, he looked... Her pulse gave an erratic little flutter. There was ony one word to describe how he looked.

Magnificent.

He paused, tucked his hands into his rear pockets, and turned to look out over the rolling green lawn to the sea. The breeze ruffled his dark hair and he lifted one hand to push it impatiently back from his forehead.

Kyra's gaze flickered over him. The seams of his T-shirt strained across his wide shoulders as he stood there, hands on his narrow hips, his muscular legs planted firmly in a stance that emphasized the overwhelming power of his masculinity.

Kyra touched the tip of her tongue to her lips. If only they had met some other way. If only they'd met in a setting like this, relaxed and easy and...

Was she losing her mind completely? The setting wouldn't change the facts. Antonio Rodrigo Cordoba del Rey was like his name: aristocratic, imperious, unforgiving. He was an inflexible, cold-blooded tyrant.

Cold-blooded? No. He was hardly cold-blooded. He had held her in his arms and kissed her with a fiery Latin passion that had stolen her breath and melted her will. Kyra's throat tightened. Was it a talent he'd been born with—or had he refined the art of seduction on more women than any man had the right to possess?

Impatiently, she swung away from the window.

Who cared how many women had trooped through his life? She didn't, that was certain. All she cared about was getting through the next few days with as little contact with Señor del Rey as possible.

Her stride was swift and determined as she made her way across the bedroom to the bath, detouring past the shards of porcelain that lay on the tile floor, all that remained of the clock she'd hurled at Antonio the night before.

Let it lie there, she thought with a toss of her head. Antonio's poor wretch of a housekeeper could deal with cleaning it up. She'd be damned if she would!

Briskly, she stripped off the bra and panties she'd slept in, tossed them onto a chair outside the bathroom, and stepped into the shower.

Sleeping in the underwear she'd worn all day—and would have to wear again, she thought, her nose wrinkling with distaste—had not been appealing. But it was better than sleeping in the raw.

She knew it was silly. After all, there'd been a locked door between her and Antonio all night. And she hadn't really feared he'd try to force himself on her. Oh, she'd taunted him about kidnapping, sure, but even while she'd done it, she'd known without question that for a man like him, the very thought was ridiculous.

Antonio del Rey had a list of faults as long as her arm, but he'd never take a woman against her will. He wouldn't have to when he had a much more effective method of guaranteeing surrender. He'd used it on her, kissing her until she'd felt as if she were drowning in a torrent of passion.

"Dammit," she said sharply, and blanked out the shameful memory. He'd never have gotten anywhere if she'd been herself. The incident was over and done with; there was no sense dwelling on it.

Kyra shut off the water. The bathroom, a huge marble-and-glass affair, had every convenience. She'd been too weary and upset to notice last night, but now, wrapped in an oversize bath sheet, she poked and sniffed among the glass vials and jars of lotions, powders and creams.

Evidently, women guests were not a rarity in this house—though she could not imagine a woman staying here. Antonio would want her in his room, in his bed. It was what the woman would want, too, to lie beside him through the long, dark night, to awaken in his arms with the heat of the sun and the heat of his kisses stirring her to arousal....

What nonsense! Kyra glared at her reflection in the mirrored wall.

"You are in desperate need of a caffeine fix," she said grimly. Her reflection nodded in agreement and Kyra grinned, scooped a white velour robe from the back of the door, and slipped it on. Still smiling, she fluffed her damp hair and walked into the bedroom.

"Good morning."

Antonio was sitting on the unmade bed, his back propped against the headboard, his hands laced lazily behind his head and his feet crossed at the ankles.

The sight of him stunned her. She gaped at him as if he'd materialized from a magician's hat.

"I trust you slept well?"

It was hard to swallow, to force her lips to move, but finally she did.

"How—how did you get in here?"

"Does it matter?"

"Of course it matters! The door was locked. And what happened to your housekeeper? She was supposed to wake me, not you!"

He shrugged lazily. "Dolores was busy so I decided to do the job myself." His sapphire gaze moved slowly over her. "Not that you needed to be awakened, I see."

A flush rose in her cheeks. The robe was heavy and long; she knew he couldn't see anything but her bare toes and yet she felt as if she were standing naked before him.

"I should have figured you'd have a key to this room, Antonio. And I should have known you wouldn't hesitate to use it."

"Ah, *querida*, your words wound me." His tone was light and teasing, as was his smile. "I have no key—but then, the door has no lock. None that works, at any rate." He chuckled as he swung his long legs to the floor. "I suppose I should have told you that."

"Yes," Kyra said stiffly, "I suppose you should have. You should also learn that if a door is shut, you're supposed to knock on it and wait until you're asked to enter."

"Another false accusation." Antonio rose to his feet and came slowly toward her. "I did knock, several times. But there was no answer."

"Of course there wasn't. I was in the shower. Didn't that occur to you?"

"It did, in fact." His eyes drifted over her again, more slowly this time, lingering all too long on the thrust of her breasts beneath the velour. "I thought, she is probably taking a shower. And when she is done, she will come back into the bedroom, her skin damp and smelling of—is that lilac?"

Kyra's heart thundered. To take a backward step, to retreat an inch, would be to show him that she was afraid. And she wasn't. There was nothing to be afraid of. Hadn't she just convinced herself of that?

"It's soap," she said coldly, her chin elevated to an almost impossible angle. "And you can save the sweet talk. I'm not impressed."

Antonio smiled. "Perhaps my gift will impress you more than my words."

"I'm trying to tell you, you're wasting your time. I'm not interested."

"Is that so?" His shoulders lifted in an easy shrug. "It was Dolores's suggestion. She thought you would like a change of clothes." He turned away and reached for something on the bed, a small, neat bundle she hadn't noticed before. "No matter. I will take what I brought you and—"

"Wait a minute." Her hand shot out, landed lightly on his arm. His skin was warm and firm to the touch, the hair on it soft and silky. Kyra snatched her hand back and stuffed it into the pocket of the robe. "I—I didn't realize you meant that you'd brought me clothing."

Antonio turned toward her. "Did you expect jewels?" He was still smiling, but there was a sudden coldness in his eyes. "But a woman like you must have all the jewels she could possibly want." He looked at her for a long moment and then he shrugged and handed the bundle to her. "These things will not be a perfect fit but they were the best I could manage on short notice."

Kyra thought of Dolores, who was at lease five inches shorter and probably eighty pounds heavier.

"That's all right," she said as she began unfolding the garments. "I don't much care about being a fashion plate. I just want to feel cle—" Her words choked to a halt. Her head came up and her gaze shot to Antonio's. "This doesn't belong to Dolores," she said, holding out a pair of faded shorts.

"No. It does not. It is mine. All the things I brought are mine."

"Yours? But—but—"

"But what? Anything of Dolores's would have been impossible. You are far too slender to wear her skirts or dresses. I would think it will be far simpler to pin the waist." He hesitated. "But if you prefer..."

"No." Kyra swallowed dryly. It was silly to be so uncomfortable at the thought of feeling his clothing against her skin. She managed a small, polite smile. "You're right. Actually, I've worn men's denims lots of times."

Antonio's answering smile was even more polite. "I see."

Her eyes flashed. There'd been a world of judgment in those two words. She knew what he thought he saw and she didn't like it.

"No," she said coldly, "you do not see. Men's clothing is not my idea of morning-after attire. What I meant was that I grew up with three brothers. I used to snag their old jeans for my own."

"Snag?" Antonio frowned. "I do not know the word."

"I used to snitch them. Borrow them . . . sort of." She bit back a smile as she remembered the nifty stack of comfortable old Levi's she'd collected before her brothers figured out what was happening. "My father didn't approve of girls wearing jeans, so until I was old enough to stand up to him—"

"I am not surprised to hear that you did not like following rules."

"Rules made arbitrarily aren't rules," Kyra said sharply. "They're commands."

Antonio's dark eyebrows rose in amusement. "Is there a difference?"

"Of course there's a difference! No one should have to obey blindly. It's—it's inhuman to expect people to do that."

His smile faded. "And that is what I am? Inhuman?"

It was on the tip of her tongue to say yes, that was precisely what he was . . . but it wasn't quite true. Would a man who was inhuman have gone out of his way to save a pair of puppies from their fate? Would such a man have faced down a knife-wielding drunk to save the neck of a strange woman?

She shrugged her shoulders. "No," she said stiffly. "I suppose not."

He laughed softly. "And I suppose that is as close as I will come to a thank-you for bringing you this designer wardrobe."

She couldn't help smiling. "Compared to the thought of putting on what I wore yesterday, it's haute couture." She took a breath. "Thank you for the clothes."

The ghost of a smile curled across his lips. "You are welcome."

Kyra stared at him. He was standing so close that she could see herself reflected in the pupils of his eyes. Two Kyras looked back at her, each with a strange, fevered look.

She swallowed hard. "Is that it?"

Antonio reached out and touched a strand of hair that lay curled against her cheek.

"Is that what?" he said, his eyes on hers.

"Is that—is that what you came to do?"

His gaze dropped to her mouth, then returned to her eyes.

"What more would you like me to do?"

His voice was soft and suddenly husky; it drifted across her skin like smoke. She took an inadvertent step back.

"I—I only meant that if you've finished talking, I'd like to get dressed."

"What a pity," he said softly. "That you wish to get dressed, I mean. I would much prefer you to stay as you are."

"Antonio," Kyra said, trying for a forceful tone. "I know you may find this intrusion very amusing, but—"

"Not amusing, *querida*. Illuminating."

His fingers stroked across her cheek, following the line of her jaw to her throat. He was touching her gently, yet somehow she could feel a pulse of flame trail behind his caress.

"Don't—don't do that," she said.

"Do what?" His brows rose. "Touch you, you mean?"

"Yes." Her breath hitched as his hand curled lightly around her throat. "I don't—I don't like it."

He smiled, but his eyes weren't smiling. They had grown dark and hot.

"Is that the reason I can feel your blood leap here, in the hollow of your throat?"

It was true; she could feel the pounding of her heart beneath the gentle pressure of his thumb. There was no sense in denying it.

"Antonio..." She searched for the words that would protect her, not from him but from whatever darkness was sweeping away her reason. "Antonio, I'm not—"

"Not what?"

"I don't—I don't want you to do this. Please. You asked me a little while ago if—if I thought you were inhuman, and—"

"Ah, *querida*, that is the problem. I am very much human when I feel the way your skin heats at my touch." He moved even closer. "And when I see the way your head tilts back just so, and your lips part..." A tremor went through her as he lifted her chin. "I am so human that I think she longs for my kiss, just as I long for hers."

"No," Kyra whispered.

His lips moved over hers in a touch as light as the brush of a butterfly against the petal of a flower. The breath sighed from her lips as he drew back and looked down at the flush on her beautiful face.

She was right; he should not do this. It was surely not what he had come here to do.

Dolores had told him, in tones of crisp disapproval, that it was obvious to anyone but a fool that the *gringa* in the guest room needed a change of clothing and he'd realized she was right.

"I will bring her something," his housekeeper had said, and Antonio had bitten his lip to keep from smiling and said no, no, he would find something for Señorita Landon himself.

And so he had come to the door and knocked. And then he'd opened it, seen the rumpled bedclothes, the wisps of silk so carelessly discarded at the bathroom door. He'd heard the drumming of the water in the shower and somehow it had become mingled with the drumming of the blood in his veins and he had told himself that to wait for her would do no harm.

He lifted his hand and drew it over her soft, shining hair. She didn't move but she made a little sound and he saw the flicker of her dark, thick lashes. She was like a cat, he thought, a cat that longed to lift its head to the soft stroke of a hand.

This was crazy. It was stupid.

Then why this rush of blood each time he touched her? Why this need to draw her tightly into his arms, to seize her mouth with his and plumb its sweet depths?

There was only one way to get her out of his system. He had to take her, bury himself in her until he was sated. And he could have her. Despite her angry words, her heated denial, he could see the truth in her silver eyes, feel it in the soft compliance of her body.

His hands cupped her face. "I have wondered," he whispered, "are you everywhere the color of the sun?" His hands swept into her hair as he lifted her face to his. "Or is your body like cream, *querida*, where the sunlight has not touched it?"

He heard the swift hitch of her breath, felt her sway unsteadily. His gaze fell to her mouth. He saw her lips part. She whispered his name and suddenly she was in his arms.

He kissed her until her mouth was soft and swollen, and his hands went to the sash of her robe. She made no move to stop him, thank heavens, for he no longer knew if he could be stopped. His control, the control he so prided himself on, was gone. His body was tensing into a sword of hard steel; he had never felt such an urgency in his life and yet he wanted to take hours to touch her, to explore her, to watch as her eyes flashed with bright silver fires.

They were smoldering now, he saw, as he undid her robe and slowly drew it from her shoulders. His hands trembled; he yearned to look down and see if her breasts

were as perfect as he knew they must be but he wanted
to watch her face as he caressed her.

"Antonio," she said fiercely. "Antonio, please..."

It was a different plea she made now, one that was
almost his undoing. He slipped his hands under her robe,
slid them down her spine and cupped her bottom; he
lifted her up into the cradle of his thighs so that she
could feel the full power of his arousal.

A cry broke from her throat and he bent and took her
mouth with his. He thrust his tongue between her lips,
telling her without words what his body would feel like
in hers, and as his heat conquered her will and filled her
senses, Kyra admitted the truth to herself. She had
wanted Antonio, wanted him to sheathe himself inside
her and ride her until the skies exploded around them
from the very first night they'd met.

He was moving against her, his erection hard against
her belly, his hands holding her face captive for his kisses.
And she was going crazy in his arms, making little sounds
she had never dreamed a woman would make, drawing
his tongue into her mouth as she struggled to get closer
and closer to him.

Nothing had prepared her for this. The books she'd
read, the whispers shared with girlfriends, the clumsy
groping she'd permitted the boys she'd grown up
with...none of it had hinted at the reality of what was
happening to her now.

How could she know that the feel of a man's mouth—
of Antonio's mouth—would make her breasts ache?
How could she know that his touch would make her flesh
quicken? She was turning to fire, to hot liquid fire that
pooled in that deepest, most feminine part of her.

She had never imagined making love could be like this.

Of course she hadn't. She had never met a man like
Antonio before. She was being seduced by an expert—

an expert who had said he'd rather take a vow of chastity than take her to his bed.

The realization stunned her and she went rigid in his arms while her fevered brain fought for control of her flesh. Antonio had come here to do this. To seduce her. To conquer her. To punish her with the ultimate humiliation.

And she had almost let him.

She swung her fists against his shoulders, taking him by surprise.

"Damn you," she said. "Let go of me!"

Sharp satisfaction swept through her as he stumbled back. The astonishment in his face made what she'd just gone through almost worthwile. It was so obvious! He'd come here to do something despicable, and she had stopped him.

"*Querida*," he said, "what is it?"

"Give it up, Antonio." Her hands shook with anger as she clasped the edges of her robe together. "That passionate Latin-lover routine doesn't work on me."

He was looking at her as if she'd lost her mind. Well, she almost had. When she thought of what she'd come close to letting him do...

"Is this how you get your women? By bringing them here and—and... Don't you know when a woman wants you to stop?"

The flush of passion was fading from his cheeks. He looked at her steadily, his eyes unreadable. The only sign of distress she could see in his face was the twitch of a tiny muscle in his jaw.

"If that is how you tell a man to stop," he said, his voice almost toneless, "then I would be interested in knowing what it is you do to tell him to continue."

"All right." She cleared her throat. "Okay. Maybe I—maybe I gave the impression I wanted you to—to kiss me. But—"

"But?" he said, his eyes on hers.

"But I didn't want anything else."

Antonio laughed. "You're a liar."

"Go on, tell yourself that, if it's what your ego needs."

"Shall I prove it to you?" He moved toward her, his face grim, and she almost stumbled in her rush to back away. A smile curled across his mouth. "Now, which of us is the liar, *querida*?"

"All right. I admit, I—I responded to you. So what? I've responded to lots of other men." The lie was so enormous that she almost gagged saying it, but it worked. Antonio couldn't manage that conceited smile this time. "I suppose I just wanted to see if a man like you could—could—"

"You wanted to see if a man like me could what?"

She stared at him while she groped for an answer. To admit that he'd almost seduced her was out of the question. But she had to say something, so she said the first thing that popped into her head.

"Look, I was curious, okay? I wanted to see if—if you could excite me."

"And?" His voice was ominously soft.

"And I found that you could. But—but the thought of doing anything else—I mean, when I thought about what I was doing, who I was doing it with—"

She cried out as his hands bit into her shoulders. "For a woman wearing nothing but a robe," he said, "you are either very stupid or very brave."

The threat brought a rush of crimson to her face and the shadow of fear to her eyes.

The sight pleased Antonio. He was not a man who enjoyed frightening women but this was different. The Kyra Landons of this world had to know they could not go through life playing games with the peasants without paying a price.

He let go of her, stalked to the bed, and snatched up the clothing he'd left there.

"Get dressed," he said sharply, tossing the bundle at her feet. "When you are ready, come downstairs and Dolores will put you to work." He paused at the door, looked down at the remains of what had once been a very expensive French clock, and edged them aside with the toe of his sneaker. "And clean up that mess. There is no one here to do it for you."

"Get out," she said, her voice trembling. "Damn you, Antonio, get out!"

He looked at her and gave her a slow, cool smile.

"With the greatest of pleasure. By the way, I would be remiss if I did not tell you that the failure of your little 'experiment' was not entirely your responsibility."

He saw her fight against asking him to explain. Her chin lifted, and he knew it was a battle she had lost.

"Is that supposed to have some deep meaning?"

He laughed. "There is nothing deep about it, *querida*. The simple fact is that I could have taken what you offered. A man would have to be a fool not to." He let his gaze move slowly over her, from the top of her head to the tips of her toes and then up again. "But it would not have been a memorable experience for me, Kyra. Do you understand? You are beautiful and desirable—but you are hardly unique."

He heard something hit the door almost as soon as he shut it. Whatever she had thrown this time, it was larger than the clock. A lamp, most probably, he thought, and despite his anger, he laughed.

She had courage, he had to give her that.

Antonio's mouth hardened.

In a little while, he would find out just how far that courage would take her.

CHAPTER SEVEN

DRESSED in Antonio's denim shorts, his T-shirt and her slightly battered thong sandals, Kyra was ready to face the day.

The shorts were baggy and the shirt hung halfway down her thighs and could have housed a family of five within its voluminous folds, which was fine because it meant she'd been able to wear nothing under it but her skin. The thought of putting on her unwashed bra and panties had made her shudder, so she'd rinsed them out and hung them over the shower door to dry.

There wasn't a way in the world anyone could possibly guess she had left off her underthings. Still, she was suddenly, almost painfully aware of her body as she stepped from the bedroom. Her breasts felt sensitized to the soft brush of Antonio's shirt; the denim shorts whispered against her flesh as she walked.

Her legs felt terribly long and bare despite the fact that the cuffs of Antonio's shorts ended just above her knees. The truth was that when she wore almost any of the designer dresses handing in her closet back home, she showed more skin than she was showing now.

Kyra frowned. She was being ridiculous. This was as unattractive and sexless an outfit as a woman could possibly wear. Besides, with any luck at all, the only person she'd see the rest of the day would be Dolores.

Briskly, she shut the door behind her and made her way down the wide staircase.

Her footsteps slowed when she reached the ground floor. Last night, the only thing she'd noticed about the

house was its enormity. Now she could see that it was
more than big; it was beautiful, too. White stucco walls
soared to meet sweeping cathedral ceilings. There were
green plants everywhere and great expanses of glass let
in the bright tropical sun. The furnishings comp-
lemented the architecture; everything was clean-lined,
simple and handsome.

It was impossible not to contrast the house with the
one she'd grown up in. The Landon mansion was a testament to wealth and power. This place was something
very different. Antonio apparently understood what
made a house a home.

Which only proved how deceptive appearances could
be, Kyra thought, giving herself a little shake. This house
might be his home but it was her prison.

The kitchen was huge, bright with sunshine and with
a dizzying variety of potted flowering plants. Sliding glass
doors looked out onto a wide brick patio.

Kyra paused uncertainly. She'd expected to find
Dolores standing by, ready to give her her marching
orders, but the room was empty. She shrugged, then
headed for the pot of coffee sitting on the stove. There
was a pair of brightly colored ceramic mugs alongside.
She filled one to the brim with the rich, dark brew and
took a long, fortifying sip.

Mmm. It was ambrosial. Antonio's housekeeper might
be a head-bobbing slave to a cold-blooded tyrant, but
she could make a terrific cup of—

The patio door slid open. Kyra turned around just as
Dolores stepped into the kitchen. A straw basket was
hooked over her arm, overflowing with tomatoes, onions
and green and red peppers. Her dark brows rose at the
sight of Kyra, but she smiled politely.

"*Buenos días, señorita.*" She slid the door shut, put
the basket down, and bustled to the refrigerator. "I am
sorry to have kept you waiting. If you will tell me, please,

how you prefer your—your. . ." She paused, and Kyra could see her struggling for the right word. "*Ay, cómo se llama heuvos?*"

"They are called 'eggs'," Kyra said in Spanish. Her tone was cool but polite. "I speak your language, Dolores. Last night, you talked to Señor del Rey as if I were not present, but I assure you, I am perfectly capable of understanding every word you say."

Dolores's black eyes were unapologetic.

"I had no way of knowing you spoke our language, *señorita*," she said stiffly. "If I offended you, I apologize."

Kyra returned the unflinching look for a moment and then she blew out her breath.

"I'm sorry. I don't know why I'm letting my anger out on you. You're only a slave here, the same as me."

The housekeeper smiled uncertainly. "Pardon?"

"Never mind. I've no right to drag you into this." Kyra put down her mug and put her hands on her hips. "Well, I'm yours to command."

Dolores's smile grew even more uneasy. "*Señorita?*"

"What do you want me to do? Scour the commodes? Hose down the stables?" Kyra threw out her hands. "Dust? Scrub? Sweep? Just tell me and I'll get started."

The housekeeper was looking at her as if she'd lost her mind.

"If you would just tell me what it is you wish for breakfast, Señorita Landon—"

"Call me Kyra. And I'll make my own breakfast, if you point me in the right direction."

Dolores looked aghast at the suggestion. "Please, *señorita*, go into the dining room. I'll bring everything to you."

"I am not a guest here, Dolores. Didn't your boss tell you that?"

"Not a guest? I do not understand. If you are not the Señor's guest, then what—"

"Señorita Landon is here as my employee."

Kyra spun toward the doorway. Antonio was standing just inside the room, hands on his hips, legs apart.

"And you are not to wait on her," he said coldly. "She will take her own meal, and then you will put her to work."

Dolores blanched. "*Señor, por favor*, I cannot possibly—"

"You may assign her whatever tasks you wish, though I suspect she will prove useless at all but the simplest things. Perhaps she can learn to scrub floors."

Kyra didn't think. She simply reacted and flung her half-full coffee mug at his head. It smashed into the wall beside him with a satisfying thunk and an even more satisfying shower of dark brown drops.

For an instant, nothing happened. Then Dolores crossed herself and muttered a prayer in Spanish, but Antonio's sharp oath drowned it out. He was across the room before Kyra could move, his eyes almost black with anger, his fingers steely as they wrapped around her shoulders.

"You will not improve your lot here if you continue playing the spoiled brat, Kyra."

"There's no way my lot can improve until I've seen the last of you!"

Antonio's eyes flashed. Slowly, he released his grip on her.

"Clean up that mess."

Dolores stepped forward. "No, no, there is no need. I shall—"

"Clean it up, I said."

Kyra put her hand on the housekeeper's arm. "There's no reason for you to do it," she said, her eyes never leaving Antonio's. "I just wish my aim had been better."

"Be grateful that it was not," he said sharply. He watched as Kyra began picking up pieces of broken pottery and then he turned to Dolores. "Remember what I said, Dolores. If Señorita Landon is to have a roof over her head and food in her belly, she must earn it."

It was, Kyra thought as she dumped the remnants of the mug into the waste bin, a hell of an exit line. Dolores apparently thought so, too.

"What is going on?" she whispered, her eyes wide. "What is he talking about?"

"He's talking about being a brute," Kyra said furiously. "What a bastard he is!"

"No! *Señorita*, you must not say such things." Dolores ripped a paper towel from the roll over the sink and wet it under the faucet. "The Señor is a good man. I have never seen him like this before."

Kyra snatched the towel from Dolores's hands and wiped up the spilled coffee.

"That's because you let him get away with demanding something instead of asking for it. You could get a better job than this anywhere! Why do you put up with his intimidation?"

"You are wrong. Truly, Señor Antonio is most kind."

"Yeah." Kyra rose, tossed the paper towel away, and marched to the stove. "And I'll bet his ancestors were the conquistadores that spread that same kindness all through South America."

"It is possible, I suppose." Dolores took a pan of sweet rolls from the warming oven. "His father was Castilian. But his mother's people were descended from the Mayans."

"The Mayans? Really?"

Dolores nodded. "*Sí*. They were of my village."

Kyra took a roll, broke it in two, and popped a piece into her mouth.

"You've known him for a long time, then," she said. The housekeeper nodded. "Where did he grow up? In Spain or in South America?"

Dolores's lips clamped shut. She swung away and began removing tomatoes from the basket she'd brought in.

"I am sorry, *señorita*. I have work to do."

A Castilian father and an Indio mother, Kyra thought, licking sugar frosting from her fingertips. That would explain a lot. Antonio's height and build were Spanish, and those eyes the color of the sea could only have come from across the ocean. But the high cheekbones, the olive skin, the hair black as night...

It was a combination that made for a man of rare physical beauty and even rarer passions. All that aristocratic insolence mixed with all that fiery passion...

Kyra frowned, shoved aside the rolls, and wiped her hands on the seat of her shorts.

"Okay," she said briskly, "tell me what my chores are. Come on, Dolores, don't look at me like that. You heard the voice of our master. If you don't put me to work, he's liable to have us both drawn and quartered."

She smiled, and after a bit, Dolores smiled, too.

"Well, perhaps you would be so kind as to empty the dishwasher...?"

"Empty the dishwasher." Kyra nodded. "And then?"

"And then—then, if you wish, you might cut up some onions and peppers. For dinner, *sí*?"

Kyra nodded again. "No problem."

It didn't take long for Kyra to decide that she was wrong. The seemingly simple job was definitely a problem.

It wasn't as if she'd never cut up vegetables before. Stella had always been proprietorial about her kitchen but there had been times she'd let Kyra help out with cutting or chopping or rolling or baking.

But this was a truly miserable job. She hadn't even touched the peppers yet, but the onions—stronger than any onions had the right to be—were making her cry. Sniffling, snuffling, rubbing the back of her wrist across her nose and her eyes, Kyra felt every bit as useless as Antonio had predicted she'd be.

Which, she thought, taking another swipe at her leaking nose, only made it all the more important to complete the job. She shot a quick look at Dolores, whose back was toward her. Then, jaw locked, she went on slicing and chopping. And suffering.

Long moments later, Dolores wiped her hands on her apron and turned to her.

"There," she said, "I have finished preparing the beef. Now..." Her eyes widened in horror. "Oh, *señorita*, what has happened to you? You are crying!"

Kyra swiped her hair back from her forehead and tried to smile.

"I'm not crying."

"You are! *Ay, caramba*, I will kill the Señor with my bare hands for making you so unhappy!"

"Really," Kyra sobbed, "I'm not crying. It's the onions."

"It is the chili peppers! I should have realized that your skin is not accustomed to their heat." Dolores yanked open the freezer door, took out a bucket of ice cubes, and dumped them into the sink. "Quickly, *señorita*. Plunge your hands into the ice."

"But I haven't even touched the chilies yet. Dolores, really—"

"By the bones of my ancestors, what is going on here?"

Antonio's angry roar filled the kitchen. Dolores turned to him, her face harsh with anger.

"The Señorita has hurt herself, and you are to blame."

"Me? I am to blame because she is incompetent?"

Antonio's angry words ground to a halt. He felt as if a fist had reached into his chest and were crushing his heart.

Kyra's beautiful face was wet and swollen with tears; she was leaning over the sink, her hands buried in ice, sobbing as if she were in agony.

God in heaven, what had happened? What had his anger and his damnable pride done to her?

He crossed the room in a couple of swift strides, pushed Dolores out of the way, and clasped Kyra's shoulders.

"What is it, *querida*?" Gently, he took her hands and lifted them from the ice, girding himself for a gusher of crimson blood or the sight of raw, burned flesh. He didn't realize he'd been holding his breath until it rushed from his lungs in relief. Kyra's hands were as they'd always been: feminine, graceful, the fingers long and graceful, the nails a pale, delicate pink.

Antonio clasped those hands in his and drew her to him.

"Kyra," he said urgently. "*Querida*, where are you injured?"

Tears flowed down her face. "I'm not," she sobbed.

His face darkened. "How can you go on being so damnably stubborn at a moment like this? Dolores! Tell me what happened!"

Dolores made a helpless gesture. "She was helping me prepare dinner."

"Did she cut herself? I see no blood."

"The chilies burned her. And the onions—"

Antonio's jaw knotted. "She scalded herself! Where? *Madre de Dios*, Dolores, where is the injury?"

"Dammit," Kyra said furiously, "you're doing it again! I'm perfectly capable of being part of this conversation, Antonio, and I'm trying to tell you, I'm not burned or cut or anything else."

"Then why are you weeping?"

"I'm *not* weeping! It's these miserable onions. They've made my eyes tear. Is that so hard to understand?"

Antonio went very still. "Let me understand this," he said in crisp English. "You are crying your heart out over a cutting board filled with vegetables?"

Her chin came up. "*You* try slicing and dicing for a while, Your Lordship!"

He could feel the adrenaline still pumping furiously through his veins. Damn this woman! Did it never occur to her to speak up and say she was in trouble? How dare she be so haughty and impertinent when he was trying to help?

His mouth twitched. And how could she have the brass to be so outrageous when her small, straight nose was pink and damp, when her beautiful silver eyes were glittering with tears?

His mouth twitched again, and Kyra gave him a look as cold as the cubes in the sink.

"What's so funny?"

"Nothing," Antonio said quickly. "Nothing is funny."

"Good. Because I want to get back to work before you decide to add time to my sentence to make up for this little interruption!"

Antonio sighed. "Forgive me for imposing Señorita Landon on you, Dolores. I should have known better."

"Yes," Dolores said. "You should have. Of all things, to treat a woman with such discourtesy..."

The housekeeper was still grumbling as Antonio led a protesting Kyra through the sliding doors and out to the patio.

"Where are you taking me?"

"Where I can keep my eye on you."

She glared up at him as he maneuvered her down the patio steps and through the garden. "What's the matter? Are you afraid I'm going to sue you?"

"I made a mistake," he said calmly. "I should have assessed your skills before turning you loose in my house."

"I have no skills, remember? You said so yourself."

"Perhaps I was mistaken."

"Hah! The great Antonio Rodrigo Cordoba del Rey, mistaken? I didn't think that was possible."

Antonio pushed open a wooden door and shoved Kyra ahead of him. Familiar smells—horse, leather and hay—filled her nostrils.

"Keep your voice down," he said coldly. "You will frighten my horses."

"Well, isn't that sweet? You don't want your horses to be upset."

"That is correct. Arabians have delicate dispositions."

"You should have told me you had horses," Kyra snapped, wrenching free of his hand.

"Why?" He smiled nastily. "You are not here to spend a holiday on horseback."

"I know something about horses, that's why!"

"I have no use for the pastimes of the wealthy, Kyra. My animals are not trained for dressage."

Kyra's eyes narrowed. "Isn't it interesting how you talk about the rich as if you weren't one of them?"

"It is true," he said stiffly. "I have wealth. But I was not born to it."

"Oh. And that, of course, makes all the difference?"

His jaw tightened at the sarcasm in her voice. "We are talking about you," he said, his tone icy, "not me. Tell me what you can do to earn your keep without injuring yourself."

"I can work with your horses. I can groom them, muck out your stalls—"

"I employ men to do that. Surely you know how to do something else."

"What?" she demanded. "Something useful? You said it yourself, Antonio. I don't know a damned thing that's useful, unless you need somebody who knows whether it's better to serve a cabernet or a Pinot Noir with beef Wellington!"

She was angrier than Antonio had ever seen her. Two spots of color had crept into her cheeks; her eyes glittered like bright silver ice after a winter rain.

Suddenly, a hunger so fierce it frightened him seized his heart. He had to get out of here, he had to get outside where there was air to breathe, where Kyra's proximity, her softness and her femininity, wouldn't drive him insane as they seemed to be doing now.

How could a woman with tearstained eyes, a woman dressed in a shirt and shorts heaven only knew how many sizes too big, look so beautiful? So desperately, incredibly desirable?

"You are in my way," he said brusquely, and shouldered past her.

Kyra was right on his heels.

"What's the matter, Antonio? Are you starting to think you ended up with a bad bargain?" She sidestepped around him, danced backward down the aisle as she kept up her taunting tirade. "I could have told you that you wouldn't find any use for an overbred, underedcuated, absolutely useless—"

Antonio reached out, grabbed her, and shook her hard.

"Shut up," he said furiously, "just shut the hell..."

With a desperate groan, his mouth fell on hers.

Kyra's reaction was instinctive. She jerked back, or tried to. But Antonio's arms swept around her, crushing her to him.

"This is what you are best suited to," he said fiercely. "You belong in my arms and in my bed, and you know it."

"No! Damn you, Antonio—"

"I am already damned," he said thickly. "Damned with wanting you. Stop fighting me, stop fighting yourself. Admit it is the same for you."

"No," she said again, "no..."

His mouth took hers again in a hard, passionate kiss. Kyra went completely still—and then, with a cry of hunger, she acknowledged the desire she had tried so hard to suppress hours ago in her bedroom. Antonio was right. She wanted him as she had never imagined wanting any man.

She raised herself to him, her hands clasping his forearms, her mouth opening to his kiss.

Antonio stumbled back against the wall, taking her with him, letting his hard body support her soft, supple weight.

"Kyra," he whispered, "Kyra, *mia exquisita...*" His teeth nipped lightly at her bottom lip as his hands swept into her hair. He drew her head back, looked down into her eyes. "I want you now," he said fiercely. "I cannot wait any longer."

Kyra felt herself quicken at his harsh words. "Here?" she whispered. "In the stable?"

"*Sí.* No one will disturb us. My men are out with the horses."

"But—but—" She caught her breath as his hands swept under her shirt and cupped her naked breasts. "Antonio," she said, "Antonio..."

He swept the shirt over her head. It sailed through the air and into a corner. Her hands rose instinctively to cover her breasts, but he caught her wrists and drew her hands to her sides.

"No," he said, "no, do not hide from me, Kyra. Ah, you are so beautiful."

· Kyra held her breath, waiting as his hands let go of hers, as they lifted slowly to her breasts and cupped them, and when his thumbs moved across the pink crests, she moaned with pleasure.

"Do you like it when I touch your breasts?" he said thickly. His hands were still on her, touching and stroking, but his eyes, dark as midnight, were on her face. "Tell me what you like. Tell me what you want."

"I want...I want..." She touched the tip of her tongue to her lips. Her body had told him, and her kisses, but now she said the words that had been buried deep within her all these weeks. "Oh, Tonio," she whispered, "I want you!"

Antonio caught her to him and kissed her deeply. Then he scooped her up into his arms and carried her through the stable to a shadowed stall spread with clean, sweet-smelling hay. He let her down slowly, kissing her as he did, and then he took a folded cotton blanket from a shelf, spread it over the hay, and eased her down beside him.

"I have dreamed of this," he whispered.

She smiled. "Have you?"

"*Sí*. I have dreamed like a boy of kissing you, so." His mouth brushed hers. "Of touching your breasts." His hand drifted over her skin, caressing her until she moaned. "Of making you mine."

His fingers closed on the zipper of her shorts. It opened and his hand slid inside, his fingers moving over her belly and into the soft curls that were already damp with her need.

Kyra caught her breath as Antonio's palm closed over her.

"*Querida*. You are so hot, so wet..." His hand moved, his fingers stroked.

"Tonio," she whispered, her eyes wide, "wait."

"Kiss me," he murmured against her mouth.

She did, and while his tongue moved against hers, his hand moved against her flesh until suddenly, with a soft, wild cry, she bucked against his touch in ecstasy.

"Tonio." Her voice broke. Her hand rose, cupped his cheek. "Tonio, I never..."

He smiled, turned his face and pressed his lips to her palm. Then he drew back, pulled off his shirt, and took her in his arms again.

The feel of her skin against his was so simple, yet it was as erotic as anything he'd ever experienced. He kissed her, reveling in the taste of her mouth. Then he took her hands, kissed them, then brought them to his shoulders and drew her flattened palms down his chest while he looked into her eyes. They were dark and wide with desire. Slowly, he eased the shorts from her body.

The sight of her lying before him, naked and languid, was almost more than he could bear. She was the most beautiful woman he had ever seen. Her breasts were round and rose-tipped above a slender waist; her hips were sweetly curved and looked made to fit his hands. And the tuft of curls that guarded her femininity was a lush, deep auburn.

Antonio's muscles tensed. He ached to bury his face at that juncture of her thighs, to inhale her scent and taste the petals of the flower he knew lay hidden within her.

But he was already too close to the point of no return. He didn't want to enter her in one swift thrust and then explode within her like a boy, and that was surely what would happen if he gave in to the primal urge that was drumming its ancient beat in his blood. Instead, he kissed her mouth again, losing himself in its sweetness and its heat, and then he rose, kicked off his sneakers, and undid his zipper.

Kyra caught her breath at the soft sound of the zipper opening. Her heart cried out for Antonio's possession but her head was warning her that once she'd made love with him, her life would never be the same again.

But it was too late for rational thought. Antonio was standing before her, his eyes as blue as the sea, his face flushed with desire, and Kyra's heart kicked against her ribs.

He was magnificent. His shoulders were broad, his arms and torso golden and tautly muscled. His skin was satin laid over steel, and she ached to touch all of him, to see all of him.

It was as if she had spoken aloud. Antonio stripped off the shorts and stood before her, glorious in his arousal.

Her eyes flew to his and he smiled and came down beside her, whispering her name. Her gaze moved across his face, that wonderful, arrogant face, and with shattering swiftness her heart flooded with an emotion so bright, so pure, that it brought tears to her eyes.

"Sweetheart?" Antonio cupped her face in his hands. "*Mia novia*, why do you cry?"

Because I just realized that I adore you, Kyra thought, but she only shook her head and lifted her arms to him.

The gesture tore into Antonio's heart. He kissed her passionately, then lowered himself between her thighs and with infinite slowness began sheathing himself in her slick heat.

Sweat beaded his skin. He could feel his breath rasping in his throat. He wanted to go slowly, to see Kyra tumble over that precipice again before he followed.

But he couldn't wait. His need was too great. He had to claim her at last, to bury himself inside her and go with her into that dark, starswept whirlpool.

With a groan, Antonio thrust forward—and met the barrier of Kyra's virginity.

Every muscle in his body went rigid. He thought his heart might swell to bursting with the knowledge that

he was the first man to know the soft secrets of her
woman's flesh, the first to make her tremble in
fulfillment.

"Antonio," she sobbed, "please, please..."

Fiercely, he kissed her. Then, his mouth still on hers,
he slid his hands beneath her, lifted her to him, and
thrust home.

CHAPTER EIGHT

THE French had a saying Kyra had learned years ago from Mlle Dufour, who had been one of her language tutors.

The more things seemed to change, the more they stayed the same.

It had been Mademoiselle's favorite adage, her way of explaining everything in the world from floods to famines to why the trains didn't run on time.

Kyra would be doing her daily lesson, reading aloud from *Paris Match* or *Elle* when some item would spark Mademoiselle's interest.

"Let me see that, *chérie*," she'd say, and after a moment she'd look up, roll her eyes and say *alors*, it was obvious that there was nothing different in this world. Things seemed to change from one day to the next, but truly, they did not.

Now, as Kyra stood leaning back in Antonio's arms, watching the crimson sun begin its descent over the sea, she thought how wonderful it would be if Mademoiselle were to suddenly appear.

"You were wrong," she would say. "Oh, you were so very, very wrong."

Things could change. Things *did* change, and with heart-stopping swiftness.

A little more than a week ago, bogged down in the age-old "who-am-I, what-am-I" quest, she'd set out on a simple adventure, hoping it might somehow jolt her into figuring out where her destiny lay.

Now she knew that it lay in Antonio's arms.

Her world had changed, and all because she'd gone
to a dance recital she hadn't much wanted to attend,
booked passage on a ship she'd known nothing about,
had her purse snatched by a thief on the streets of a city
where she was a stranger....

A soft laugh bubbled in her throat.

Antonio drew her closer into his arms. "What is this?"
His tone was gruff but she could feel his lips curve into
a smile as he pressed them lightly to her temple. "The
tourist office would be appalled to know that the sight
of the sunset makes my Kyra laugh."

My Kyra. Her heart seemed to repeat the magical
words and she smiled and tilted her face to his.

"What tourist office? We rode our horses the length
of this island today and I didn't see anything but sun
and sea and sky."

Antonio grinned. "You are a very observant woman,
Señorita Landon. Have I told you that?"

"I don't think so. All I recall your saying is that I'm
a danger in the kitchen but that I have an excellent seat."

"Indeed." His smile tilted as he turned her in his arms.
His hand slid down her back and gently cupped her
bottom. "Actually, I should have said you have an
extraordinary seat. One I will never tire of admiring."

Kyra laughed and wound her arms around his neck.
"I was talking about my riding technique, *señor.*"

"*Sí.*" Antonio's eyes darkened. "As was I."

His soft words sent a flood of color racing into her
cheeks. She gave a soft laugh and buried her face in his
throat.

"Hush, Antonio. Dolores might hear you."

"Dolores is in the kitchen, preparing a feast she will
pretend is the light supper I requested." Smiling, he put
his arm around Kyra and they began walking slowly
along the gravel path that led through the garden. The
dogs, Bashful and Dopey, yawned, got to their feet, and

loped on ahead. "My housekeeper is a happy woman, thanks to you."

Kyra looked up at him and smiled. "I'll bet she is. She probably had visions of my bringing her kitchen down around her ears."

Antonio thought of what Dolores had said to him just that morning, that she had despaired of ever seeing him so happy. But it was too much to admit, even though he knew in his heart it was the truth. He was not ready to give so much of himself away, to trust so completely.

"*Sí.*" He bent his head and kissed Kyra's upturned face. "She thanked me for getting you out from under her feet. I said it was a sacrifice but one any man would make to be certain his meals were served on time."

He laughed as Kyra swung out in front of him and mimed a look of fierce indignation.

"And here I thought you were about to give me a compliment! I suppose I should have known bet—"

Her breath caught as Antonio swept her into his arms and kissed her passionately.

"You have made me happy, too, *querida*," he said softly, framing her face in his hands. "Is that a compliment more to your liking?"

"You know it is."

"And is it one you can return?"

Kyra smiled into his eyes. "I'm happier than I've ever been in my life."

Antonio lifted her face to his. "Is this true?"

"Yes. Oh, Tonio, I..."

"What? What were you going to say, sweetheart?"

That I love you.

The words were there on the tip of her tongue, but she couldn't bring herself to say them. If only Antonio would say them first, if only he would take her in his arms and kiss her and say, Kyra, *mia querida*, I adore you.

"Kyra?" In the gathering darkness, Antonio's eyes were as deep and unfathomable as the sea. "Tell me what you are thinking."

It was hard, but she managed a quick, gently teasing smile.

"Only that—that somewhere in Caracas, there's a thief who'll never know he did a good deed by snatching the purse of an unsuspecting *gringa*."

Antonio smiled, though it took some effort. What had he hoped she would say? Something more, something that would free him to tell her—to tell her...

He frowned, put his arm around her shoulders, and they began strolling through the garden again.

"*Sí*," he said. "It is strange what misfortune can sometimes bring."

Misfortune? It had been the happiest day of her life, Kyra thought as she leaned her head against his shoulder. She had found paradise.

Yesterday, after they'd made love the first time in the stable, Antonio had taken her back to the house. There, in the quiet of his room and the softness of his bed, he had made love to her again, this time with a slow thoroughness that had left her twisting in his arms, begging him to end the sweet torment.

At night, they'd dined by candlelight on the patio, Antonio incredibly handsome in a tuxedo, she feeling flushed and silly in his spruce green silk robe with the cuffs rolled back. But Antonio kept telling her how beautiful she looked.

"More beautiful than any woman I have ever known," he'd said, until she almost believed him, and if Dolores had been surprised to find that the morning's scullery maid had turned into a princess by evening, she'd hidden it well. And there'd been a curve to the housekeeper's lips that had warmed Kyra's heart.

After dinner, they'd danced on the moonlight-drenched patio. Eventually, they hadn't been dancing at all; they'd only been swaying in each other's arms, kissing and caressing and whispering until Antonio had swept her into his arms and carried her up the stairs to his room.

The night had passed in a haze of slow, tender exploration and explosive, fierce passion, and awakening in his arms this morning had been the most wonderful part of it all.

And today...Kyra's breath caught. Today, they'd saddled horses and ridden along the beach to a half-moon cove ringed by coconut palms.

"How beautiful this is," she'd said, and Antonio had said yes, she was right, she was, indeed, beautiful.

"Not me," she'd said, turning to him and laughing. "That isn't what I meant, Antonio."

But then she'd looked into his eyes, those blazing, sapphire eyes, and in a heartbeat she was in his arms and he was bearing her down beneath him to the hot, white sand.

The memory sent a shiver of pleasure racing along her skin. Antonio's arm tightened around her.

"Are you chilly, *querida*? Sometimes, at night, the breeze that comes in off the sea can be cooler than one would imagine."

"No, I'm fine. I was just thinking about..." She felt color sweep into her face. "Never mind. It's not important."

"Was it a good thought or a bad one?"

She laughed softly. "A good one, but don't bother trying to find out what. If I told you any more, you'd be insufferable."

Antonio chuckled. "I am already insufferable, according to you. Isn't that one of the things you called me over the past few days?"

''Well, you were.'' Kyra smiled. ''Insufferable, impossible, unbearable—but I suppose if you weren't, you wouldn't have dragged me off to your lair.''

Antonio turned her toward him. He stroked her hair back from her face, his fingers following the shell-like curve of her pink earlobe.

''You mean,'' he said with a little smile, ''I would not have brought you here if you had not been stubborn, foolish and altogether impossible.''

''Me? Impossible?'' Kyra laughed softly. ''You're the impossible one, Tonio, not me.''

Antonio's thumbs swept over the arc of her cheekbones.

''Say it again,'' he whispered.

''Say what again?''

''The name you call me.''

''Tonio? Isn't it all right? I mean, if you don't like me using it—''

He kissed her. ''I love you using it. It is just that no one has ever used a—what do you call the little name?''

''A nickname.'' Kyra frowned and pulled back in his arms. ''Wait a minute. No one's ever called you Tonio before?''

He laughed at the look on her face. ''Why are you so surprised?''

''What did they call you, then?''

''When?''

''Well, when you were little.''

A muscle knotted in his jaw. ''Many things,'' he said. ''But none you would call a nickname.''

''I don't understand.''

Antonio shrugged. ''It is not important.''

''But—''

''Come, tell me about yourself.'' He smiled down at her as they began walking back to the house. ''What were you called when you were a little girl?''

Kyra laughed. "What do you mean, when I was a little girl? As far as my brothers are concerned, I'll probably never outgrow being called Little Sister or Squirt."

Antonio laughed, too. "Squirt? You were squeezed out? Is that it?"

"No!" She smiled. "That's not what 'Squirt' means when it's a nickname. It refers to—to something small and insignificant."

"This is a term of affection?" he said, his brows lifting.

"If you knew Cade and Zach and Grant," she said, "you'd understand."

"You have three brothers?"

"Yes. Although sometimes, when they're busy poking their noses into my life, it feels as if it's more like a dozen."

Antonio nodded. "They are concerned for your welfare," he said. "You are fortunate, having a family that loves you."

"I know, but—"

"I had no family."

The simple words were harsh and almost without inflection. Kyra stopped walking and swung toward him.

"No family? But Dolores said—"

"What?" Antonio's tone grew sharp. "What did that foolish old woman tell you?"

"Nothing, really. Just that she and your mother came from the same village and that your father was a Spaniard."

"She talks too much, that Dolores."

"She didn't mean any harm, Antonio."

He sighed. "No," he said after a moment, "no, I suppose she did not. It is true. I had a mother and a father. But they did not raise me."

"Why? What happened to your parents?" Kyra felt Antonio stiffen beside her. "I'm sorry," she said quickly. "It's none of my bus—"

"My father was in South America on business." He shrugged. "I have the story only secondhand, from my grandmother. He and my mother met..." He shrugged again. "Perhaps he never knew he had made my mother pregnant. She gave birth to me and it was the last anyone in the village saw of her."

Kyra's throat constricted. "Oh, Tonio," she said softly, "how awful for you."

His arm dropped away from her. "I do not tell you this to ask for pity," he said coldly. "I tell it to you only because—because you asked me about my family."

She had not asked him; he had volunteered. It was a subtle difference, yet Kyra knew it somehow held a world of meaning. But there was no time to think about it, not just now. Now, she was too busy forcing herself not to put her arms around Antonio and tell him there was nothing wrong with feeling compassion, especially when you loved someone.

She cleared her throat. "I see."

But she didn't see, not at all. Who had raised him, if not his parents? Had he been given into the care of relatives? Had he been handed over to an orphanage? Whatever had happened, she was almost painfully relieved she hadn't told him about a father who'd tried to think for her or about the three big brothers who'd always made her a mascot but never a member of their silly clubs.

All of it was true, all of it had shaped her life...but how petty it would sound to a man whose childhood had lacked the love and warmth of people who cared about him.

Kyra longed to ask a dozen questions, but the set of Antonio's face warned her that this wasn't the time. Instead, she put her hand on his arm, and when he looked at her, she rose toward him and kissed his mouth.

"I wish I'd known you when you were a little boy," she said softly.

Antonio looked at her for a long moment. Then he gathered her into his arms so tightly that she could hardly draw breath.

"*Querida*," he whispered, "come to bed with me now."

Kyra felt a blush rise in her cheeks. "But—but Dolores..."

He smiled. "She has been on this earth many years. She knows how it is between lovers."

Lovers, Kyra thought, her heart lifting, lovers. It was such a beautiful, wonderful word.

"Say the other name," he murmured, his mouth inches from hers. "Let me hear it on your lips."

She smiled. "Tonio," she whispered, "my Tonio..."

He kissed her, his mouth open and hot against hers, until she was clinging helplessly to him, her hands curled into the front of his shirt.

"Come to bed, *querida*," he said thickly. "I need you now."

"Yes," she breathed, and he caught her in his arms, carried her through the house and up the stairs to his room. He kicked the door shut, and the night and the stars closed down around them.

Hours later, Antonio stirred and awoke.

It was very late, that time in the darkness when the silence of the night is as heavy as the silence of the soul. He turned his head on the pillow and gazed at Kyra, lying curled in the circle of his arm.

Gently, so as not to disturb her, he bent and brushed his lips over hers. She sighed and snuggled closer into his embrace.

It hurt his heart just to look at her. She was so beautiful. He smiled to himself. And so spirited. No woman had ever stood up to him as she had. No man, either. People had been deferring to him for a decade; he was Antonio Rodrigo Cordoba del Rey, and even if someone, somewhere, suspected the truth, that he had created himself out of a boy who had almost not grown up to become a man, that the father whose names he bore had never known or cared about his existence, what did it matter? He was wealthy, he was important...no one dared defy him.

No one but Kyra. She was the only living soul in a dozen years he had told about himself, not all of it but enough. Even the things Jessamyn had known about him had not come from his lips; her father had told her the story of Antonio's origins and—and—

And Jessamyn had almost destroyed him. Antonio's smile faded. He had thought himself in love with her. How foolish he'd been! He should have known that the lessons learned in childhood never really change. Love was a lie created by poets for fools to believe in.

Now, at thirty-two, he knew love for the hoax it was. It would be so easy to think himself in love with Kyra. She was beautiful. Vibrant. Exciting. The sound of her voice, the scent of her skin, aroused a hunger in him that could not be sated. And she had given him the gift of her virginity.

He was touched. He was happy. But he wasn't stupid enough to try to call what he felt "love".

He looked at her again, asleep in his arms. A fist tightened around his heart. No, he thought, no, this was not love. They would enjoy what they had for as long as it lasted. A week. A month. And then...

Kyra murmured in her sleep, sighed, and rolled onto her back. Antonio waited, then hiked himself up on one elbow. Slowly, he drew down the light blanket and let his eyes skim her lush, lovely curves.

The hunger that swept through him didn't surprise him. What followed—the throat-catching tenderness—did. He fought against the desire to waken her, to take her in his arms not to stir her to passion but to see her smile as her eyes focused on his face, to feel the warmth of her against his skin.

He frowned, drew the blanket over her again, and eased his arm out from beneath her shoulders. He rose from the bed, walked to the partially opened French doors opposite, and stepped out onto his balcony.

The night breeze carried the tang of the sea on its warm breath. He shut his eyes, remembering another scent, the almost overpowering smell of camellias that he had, for years, identified with Jessamyn.

Por Dios, what was wrong with him tonight? He had put Jessamyn out of his heart years ago yet tonight he couldn't get her out of his head. Antonio sighed. Perhaps it was best to let himself remember every detail. That might put the memories to rest once and for all.

A Peace Corps volunteer had plucked him from his village and a life in which he had fought for scraps like a street mongrel and brought him to a Jesuit missionary school where three meals a day, a roof over his head, and a corner to call his own had been like a little piece of heaven.

At seventeen, he'd been told that he'd won a scholarship to an exclusive American university.

A week later, he was in Boston.

He knew no one, spoke stilted, textbook English and a Spanish dialect almost incomprehensible to others. He was almost always broke. And he had an attitude that made it clear he had a very large, very precariously balanced chip on his shoulder.

One of his professors, a Boston Brahmin with a bloodline as pure as his family fortune was large, had taken pity on him. In a burst of egalitarian generosity, he took Antonio under his wing.

Within weeks, Antonio found himself absorbed into the bosom of the man's patrician family.

Or so he thought.

He blossomed. He learned to smile, to talk, to share, to let others see what the Peace Corps volunteer and the missionaries had seen—the bright mind, the clever wit lurking just under the sullen exterior.

And, inevitably, he fell in love with the professor's daughter.

Her name was Jessamyn. She was blond and terribly sophisticated. Antonio confined himself to sidelong glances and sweaty dreams. The professor was his mentor, he had no wish to do anything that would presume on the man's kindness.

But Jessamyn made such lofty ideas impossible. She touched his thigh under cover of the dining-room table; on the frequent occasions that he spent the night in the room opposite hers, she "forgot" to close her bedroom door as she prepared for bed.

Eventually, Antonio took what was so blatantly offered. In his naiveté, he assumed Jessamyn loved him just as he was sure he loved her. He added a second job to the one that was already necessary to supplement his scholarship money, saved enough to buy her a ring with a stone even he knew was painfully small, and promised himself he would someday replace it with the perfect diamond she deserved.

That was what he told her when he proposed.

Jessamyn laughed in his face.

Antonio shut his eyes against the night, the sea and the pain of that memory.

"Marriage?" she'd said. "To you? Antonio, darling, surely you know that could never happen!"

And then she lifted up her skirt, put his hand on her flesh, and shuddered with pleasure.

He left school the next day, made his way back to South America, and traded the price of the ring for the equipment he needed. Then he trekked into the jungle for months of backbreaking labor on a mining claim that was the butt of a hundred different jokes.

A year later, he knew he had never really loved Jessamyn. He was also a millionaire ten times over.

After that, he had his choice of women, all of them with blood as blue as Jessamyn's. It was interesting how a man's bank account could ultimately matter more than his lineage. Any one of his conquests would have married him, but Antonio only smiled, took what was offered, and moved on.

And then, one night in Colorado, a woman with hair the colors of autumn had flashed him a look that carried a message he had almost forgotten. Unlike the others, she hadn't cared that he had money, and power. Her silver eyes had said it all.

"I know who you really are," those eyes had said, "and what you are. And try as you like, you can't have me."

But he had had her. Antonio drew a harsh breath of the sea-scented night air. He had made love to Kyra Landon, and now, and now—now, he didn't want to let her go....

"Antonio?"

His heart lifted at the sound of that sleepy voice. He turned and found Kyra sitting up against the pillows, the blanket at her waist. The waning light of the ivory moon lay pale on her face and breasts.

Antonio's breath caught. Kyra, he thought, my Kyra.

She smiled, lifted her hand in act of unconscious sensuality and pushed her hair back from her face.

"Tonio," she said softly, "come back to bed."

Antonio looked at her. How could he think of an ending to all this? He could not. By all he held dear, he could not!

"Tonio? You look so strange...is something wrong?"

He crossed the room quickly, came down next to her in the bed, and took her in his arms.

"Yes," he whispered, "something is very wrong, *querida*. I have not made love to you in far too long."

He kissed her and moved over her, telling her with his body what he could not even tell himself.

But a long while later, as the sun rose over the rim of the sea, with Kyra sleeping in his arms, he knew it was time to stop pretending.

He, the man who scorned love, had fallen in love.

The realization terrified him.

CHAPTER NINE

KYRA woke slowly, safe and warm in Antonio's arms.

Had she ever been this happy in her life?

She didn't need to think about the answer. She knew it as surely as she knew she loved Antonio.

Smiling, she propped her head on her hand and watched him as he slept. He looked so young, so boyish. A lock of dark, silky hair had fallen over his brow; his lashes lay thick and black against his high cheekbones. And his mouth—that hard, beautifully chiseled mouth—was soft and relaxed.

Carefully, so as not to wake him, she bent and touched her lips gently to his. He made a sighing sound, his hand lifted and brushed against her hair but he didn't awaken.

"I love you," Kyra whispered.

And she did, with all her heart.

She had come to the Caribbean to find herself. And she had. She had found that she was a woman, with a woman's needs, passions and hopes; she had found what she needed to make herself complete.

She needed Antonio, and his love.

Kyra sank back against the pillows. Had she really only been on San Sebastian Island three days? It felt so much longer than that. But it was three days, which meant today was Monday.

And that meant at least a temporary return to reality.

She had to go to Caracas, contact the embassy. And the cruise line, too. For all she knew, they might have decided she'd fallen overboard!

And her banker—she had to call him. She needed funds, and why should she give a damn if he gave her a lecture? She'd simply tell him to mind his own business.

Kyra smiled. Why hadn't that occurred to her before?

But she knew the reason. It was because she'd left Denver a child in rebellion. It was why she hadn't told anyone she was leaving, why she'd recoiled at the thought of phoning home for help.

What nonsense that had been! She was an adult; she knew that now. Whatever decisions needed to be made in her life, *she* would make them. Whatever she did or didn't do was strictly her business, and she would not let anybody chastise or scold her, not her banker or her attorney or even her three beloved, impossible big brothers.

Not even Antonio.

The thought came out of nowhere, and for an instant, it paralyzed her but then she gave herself a mental shake and called herself a fool.

She knew Antonio now. He wasn't the dictatorial tyrant she'd pegged him for. He was considerate and thoughtful with his secretary and with his housekeeper; he'd stopped at nothing to help her even when they were still sniping at each other. It was just that their relationship had gotten off to a bad start.

All that was changed now. Kyra turned her head on the pillow, her expression softening as she looked at Antonio's face. Oh yes. Everything had changed....

Like a ghostly whisper, Mademoiselle's voice sighed inside her head.

The more things seemed to change, the more they stayed the same.

No. No, the old dictum wasn't true anymore.

It had been, years ago when she was a little girl. Her father would treat her brothers with something approximating kindness for a day or so, just long enough for her to let herself stupidly start to believe things were going to change.

But nothing ever did. Life would go back to what it had always been. Nothing at all would have changed.

Kyra shivered. Quickly, she shoved aside the blankets and padded into the bathroom. She turned the shower on full and stepped under it, turning her face up to the spray.

She was being silly. Antonio was nothing like her father. He wasn't selfish or self-centered. Besides, she loved him. And she was sure he loved her.

Or did he? He hadn't said so. And what would it prove if he did? Her father had loved her; it had been in the name of love that he'd all but suffocated her.

She made a sound that should have been a laugh as she turned off the water. Here she stood, agonizing over whether or not she could live the rest of her life with a man who hadn't even suggested that he wanted to live the rest of his life with her.

Hastily, before Antonio could awaken, take her in his arms and add to her growing confusion, she threw on a pair of his shorts and a shirt, slipped on her sandals, and hurried downstairs, where a surprised Dolores took one look at her face and wisely said nothing but "*Buenos días*" as she helped herself to some coffee.

Cup in hand, she made her way down to the paddock.

"Kyra?"

Antonio shot up in bed, his heart pounding. He had dreamed something—he couldn't quite remember what, only that he had once again been alone on his island, that Kyra was gone.

He swallowed hard, ran his fingers through his hair. He was not a man who believed in dreams, only in reality. And the reality was that Kyra had come into his life and he would not be fool enough to lose her.

Smiling, he rose and made his way to the bathroom, expecting to find her in the shower, expecting to slip into the steamy cubicle with her.

She wasn't there. Antonio's brows drew together. There was nowhere she could have gone. He knew that. But he thought again of his dream, and his frown became a scowl.

Suppose she wanted to leave? What would he say? He had no right to keep her here, not any longer. He had brought her here a captive; now, he was the captive. She had taken his heart.

And what will she do with it, Antonio?

He shook his head. She would not leave the island. Not now. She had told him how happy she was; why would she flee that happiness?

There was time. Plenty of time. Over the next days, the next weeks, he would tell her what he felt. He would show her, not just by making love to her but by cherishing her. By protecting her, and taking care of her. He would start this very morning, by arranging for the replacement of her passport and visa. And he would take her shopping. He smiled, thinking of how incredibly sexy she looked in his clothes. But she would want things of her own, and he would get them for her.

Finally, when the time was right, he would tell her.

I love you, *querida*, he would say, and it would be all right because she was not Jessamyn, and he was not a foolish boy any longer.

Whistling softly, Antonio stepped into the shower.

Kyra stood at the paddock behind the garden, sipping her coffee and watching Antonio's Arabians wheeling across the meadow.

Getting up early, coming down here where she could sort out her thoughts, had been a good idea.

There was no point in worrying about things in advance. She would ask Antonio to take her to Caracas, she would take the first steps toward putting her life in order, and—

A pair of strong, masculine arms closed around her.

"There you are," Antonio said. His tone was warm if slightly gruff. He turned her in his arms, tilted her face to his, and gave her a long, deep kiss. "I have looked for you everywhere, *querida*. You should have told me you were coming here to see the horses."

"You were asleep," Kyra said, smiling up at him.

"*Sí*. In that case, you should have told Dolores."

Her smile dimmed just a little. "Why?"

"Well, because—because . . ." *Because I don't know what I would do if you left me.* Antonio frowned. "I was concerned."

"About what? Nothing can happen to me here, Antonio."

She was right, of course. What he was concerned about had nothing to do with reality and everything to do with love—but how could he tell her that?

"That is true," he said stiffly, "but this is my island, and I am responsible for the welfare of everything and everyone on it."

The smile left her face altogether. "I see," she said. She drew back out of his arms and turned to the paddock again. "Perhaps I should sign in and out in the future."

Antonio winced. Stupid, he told himself, stupid! Gently, he put his hands on her shoulders.

"*Querida*," he said softly, "forgive me. It is just that— that I awakened and reached for you but you were not there. My bed suddenly was cold and lonely."

His words reached into Kyra's heart. She sighed, turned to him, and laid her hands against his chest.

"Let's start over," she said. "Good morning, Tonio."

Antonio smiled back at her. "Good morning, *querida*." He kissed her gently, then drew back, his arms still encircling her. "I have a plan."

"A plan?" She laughed softly and leaned back in his arms. "That sounds serious."

"Well, it is not serious but it is important." He flashed her a quick grin. "As much as I would like to keep you at my mercy, with no papers and no clothes, I have decided it is wrong." Antonio took her face in his hands. "I am going to take you to Caracas so you can pick up a new passport and visa."

"And clothes."

He laughed. "And clothes, *sí*." His eyes met hers. "I am hoping that even with all of those things in your hands, you will choose to stay here with me."

For how long? she thought, but she only nodded.

"You know I will."

Antonio's heart swelled. His head was full of words, but his tongue wouldn't form them. There was time. There was lots of time.

"So then," he said, "it is settled, yes?"

"Yes. And I'm glad you mentioned going to Caracas. I was going to ask you about it. I mean, I've thought of so many things that I need to take care of—"

Antonio kissed her lightly on the mouth.

"It is too early in the day for a beautiful woman to waste time thinking."

It was a gallant compliment, flowery and Latin. Still, it made her smile tilt just a little.

"I'm serious, Antonio."

"So am I. Truly, there is nothing for you to worry your beautiful head over. I have thought of everything."

She laughed. "Such modesty! What do you mean, you've thought of everything?"

"Well, as I said, though I love the way you look, dressed in my things, *querida*, I know you long for clothes of your own."

"Oh yes, I do. I'm going to telephone my bank and—"

"There is no need. I will take you shopping. Whatever you buy will be charged to my account."

"That's very generous, Antonio, but I couldn't let you do that."

"Nonsense." Antonio waved his hand in the air in that imperious gesture that had almost driven her crazy a couple of days ago. "That is how it will be. There is nothing to discuss."

"You're wrong." Kyra cleared her throat. "I think— I think there are lots of things to discuss. I appreciate what you're doing, but—"

"Sweetheart, if you wish, we can talk in the plane." Antonio looped his arm around her waist. "And I told your embassy to have your papers ready promptly at noon, and—"

"My embassy? You mean, you got in touch with them?"

"Of course."

"Yes, but—but I'm the one who lost the passport and visa—"

"And I am the one who will see to it that they are replaced." He hugged her and smiled. "You see, *querida*? There is no need for you to lift a finger. I will do it all."

"You should have asked me first, Antonio."

"Asked you what? These things had to be done, yes?"

"That isn't the point. I'm perfectly capable of—"

"*Mia querida*, is it so terrible that I wish to take care of you?"

She stared at him for a moment, and then she gave a deep sigh.

"No, of course not. But—but..." She hesitated, trying to find the right way to phrase what she needed to tell him. "The thing is, I've always had someone taking care of me, Antonio. I mean, everyone in my family's always been—"

"Protective. Yes. So you said." He smiled. "It pleases me to know that you had such love all your life. It is very Latin."

A cold hand seemed to close around Kyra's heart. "It may be Latin," she said carefully, "but my father..."

Kyra broke off and stared at him. But what? But thinking for someone else, protecting them from real life, making them live their lives as an extension of yours, wasn't love.

How could she tell him that, when she knew there had never been anyone to care for him, that he had probably seen all too much of real life? It would be like explaining the way new shoes might pinch your feet to a man with no shoes at all.

"Tonio," she said, "please try to understand. I do appreciate your concern for me. But you and I—"

"*Sí.*" Antonio looked into Kyra's beautiful eyes, and his heart turned over. Why had he thought he could wait to tell her that he loved her? The knowledge lit his soul like a flame. He wanted to tell her he adored her, to ask her to marry him, to know the joy of seeing her smile and say yes. "*Sí,*" he said again, and he took a deep breath. "You and I, Kyra. That is what I wish to talk to you about."

Kyra's heart stood still. "You?" she said, her eyes searching his. "You—and I?"

"Yes." Yes? Was that all he could manage to croak out? *Dios,* what was wrong with him? He was a fool, stumbling for words. And it wasn't necessary. She loved him; he knew that she did. He cleared his throat. "I realize we have only known each other for a few days," he said, "and that—that our backgrounds are very different."

"Yes," Kyra said quickly. She put her palms flat against his chest and felt his heart galloping beneath her fingers. "Yes, they are. That's what I'm trying to tell you. It's so complicated, Antonio, but—but I'll try to make you understand. You see, my brothers were so much older. They became very protective of me."

"Of course. I have no difficulty understanding that. What man would not feel protective of you, *querida*?"

"And my father...how can I explain? He had certain expectations for me—"

Antonio stiffened. "Expectations?"

"Yes. He had my life planned. He was determined that I only do certain things, know certain kinds of people—"

"*Sí.* I am sure he did."

"I had to live up to those expectations, Antonio. It wasn't a matter of choice." Kyra shook her head. "It's like a—a family requirement, you know? A set of commands that are never spoken, that you grow up knowing have to be obeyed for the rest of your life."

"I tell you again, I understand all of this, Kyra." He smiled, but it was not a smile that reached his eyes. "You may have grown up with privilege and I without, but that does not mean I do not believe in expectations and rules, as well."

"That's just the point! You seem to think I'd want to go from one set of rules to another."

Antonio folded his arms over his chest. "The principles that govern my life are not so different from yours. I would expect you to accept them."

Dammit, why was he being so impossible? Before her eyes, he was turning back into the cold, unyielding tyrant he'd been before they became lovers. She was trying to make him understand that she would never march to the beat of anyone else's drum again and *he* was arrogantly assuring her that she would if he were the drummer!

"Antonio," she said with forced patience, "try looking at this from my viewpoint. I grew up in this—this enormous house—"

"Ah, *sí*." He smiled coldly. "I have no difficulty imagining it, Kyra. A big house."

"Yes. A mansion."

"Filled with all the trappings of power and money."

"Exactly." She waved her hand toward his beautiful, warm home. "It was nothing like this place, Antonio, nothing at all like it."

A flush rose high on his cheeks. "I am not stupid, Kyra. The picture you paint is quite clear. You grew up a princess in a castle."

Kyra gave a little laugh. "Rapunzel?" she said. "Yes, I suppose that's one way to look at it."

A terrible coldness was forming around Antonio's heart. He wanted to reach out and pull Kyra into his arms, kiss her and kiss her until she remembered that everything she was talking about was unimportant compared to what they felt for each other.

But the truth was he had no idea what she felt for him. He had made assumptions, leaped to conclusions....

He had made that mistake before.

He turned, walked a few steps, then swung around to face her.

"None of this mattered yesterday," he said tonelessly, his eyes on her face.

Kyra sighed. "It did. It's part of the reason I was so hesitant about—about our becoming involved." *It's one of the reasons I was so afraid to admit to myself that I was falling in love with you.* The thought was so clear and sharp in her head...but this wasn't the time to speak of love, not when Antonio was standing there looking stern and unapproachable, when she was standing here knowing that she could never be herself if she allowed him to control her life. "I suppose—I suppose it would have been better if you'd known more about me before I came to your island, Antonio, but—"

"But you did not come here willingly." A muscle danced in his cheek. "I brought you here."

"Yes. And I didn't expect—I didn't expect—"

"To end up in my bed."

Kyra winced. She had meant that she hadn't expected to fall in love. Antonio's words, delivered with stoic callousness, put a very different edge on things and brought a rush of flame to her cheeks.

"That's true."

"*Sí*. It is. It is true that I brought you here, true that I gave you no choice but to come." His eyes darkened as he came toward her. "But I did not force you to make love."

"I never said you did! I'm just trying to explain why..." She blew out her breath. "I don't know how to get through to you, Antonio."

"Perhaps," he said coldly, "it would be best if you simply got to the point."

"The point," she said, flinging out her arms, "is that we have different expectations. I knew that as soon as you told me about yourself, about your childhood. I should have said something then, but I didn't want to hurt you..."

She was still talking, her silver eyes fixed on his, but Antonio was no longer listening. Why should he, when he knew what she was going to tell him? He was not good enough for her. She would say it with more kindness than Jessamyn, but the message would be the same. Despite his wealth, despite his feelings for her, she was still the princess and he was the commoner. He was good enough for the dark passion that swept over them in the night, but anything else was out of the question.

A rage so deep it drove every sane thought from his head swept through Antonio. He wanted to reach out and grab Kyra, to shake her until her bones rattled, to force her face up to his and kiss her until she cried out the truth, that the "expectations" that were so important to her would never allow her to admit that she had fallen in love with the rough-bred bastard who loved her.

But he didn't love her. He was only a victim of the same foolishness that had happened years ago.

Was he such a sentimental idiot that he could not want a woman for more than a couple of days without trying to convince himself he loved her?

"Enough," he said, his voice slicing harshly into her endless explanation.

"Antonio?" Kyra stared at him. His face had become a white mask under its olive hue; the skin was drawn so tight that it looked as if it might tear over the sharp bones beneath. "Antonio, please. Listen to me."

"I am done listening."

"I don't think you've listened at all."

"I have listened," he said with disdain, "and now I am bored."

Kyra flushed. "Bored? Bored, while I've tried to explain how we might work things out?"

His teeth flashed in a quick smile. "I know what you have proposed, Kyra. We will go on as we have been, with you in my bed."

Her flush deepened. "Well, yes. That will give us time to explore each other, and—"

Antonio laughed. "Ah, *querida*, I have explored you all that is necessary. I know what makes you moan, what makes you reach up and pull me down to you. What more exploration do I need than this?"

Kyra paled. That he should reduce things to such a level stunned her. Was this what happened when he couldn't get his own way?

Antonio saw the look on Kyra's face. He had hurt her deeply; he should have felt a rush of satisfaction. Instead, a pain lanced into his heart.

"Kyra..."

"Don't," she said. She wrapped her arms around herself. "I—I want to leave here, Antonio."

"Kyra, what I just said—"

"I don't give a damn about what you just said," she lied. Her chin lifted. "I wish to be in Caracas by this afternoon."

Antonio's eyes narrowed. "I am not a boy to be given orders."

"No." Kyra's voice trembled. "You're not a boy, Antonio. You're a coldhearted, mean-tempered, no-good—"

She cried out as his hands closed on her shoulders.

"Be careful of what you say to me," he growled.

"I'll say whatever I damned well please."

"You will not!"

"Listen, Antonio, maybe you can give orders to the rest of the world, but I won't take them!"

"But you will, *querida*." The coldness in his tone made the word anything but an endearment. "You are my servant on this island. Have you forgotten that—or did you think your performance in bed would satisfy your debt?"

Kyra felt the blood drain from her face. How could she have thought herself in love with this man? No woman could love Antonio del Rey, not if she valued her self-respect.

"Thank you for reminding me of my position here," she said, her voice trembling. "And you're right, Antonio. I haven't repaid my debt. But if there's a shred of decency in that—that block of ice you call a heart, you'll let me leave San Sebastian right away."

He nodded stiffly. "With pleasure. I will telephone for an air taxi."

He turned and walked away. By late afternoon, new passport and visa in hand, Kyra was at the airport in Caracas and on her way home.

CHAPTER TEN

IT WAS the coldest winter Colorado had seen in years.

Everyone agreed to that, from the TV weather forecasters trying not to look gleeful as they flashed satellite maps and photographs each evening to the tourists pouring into towns like Aspen and Boulder.

For her part, Kyra was too busy to notice.

She had returned from the Caribbean filled with a brisk, almost brittle, energy. Within a week's time, she had signed up for evening classes in computer science and real estate at the university and accepted chairmanship of an art exhibition that people said would be the highlight of the season.

In November, she got a call from Zach. He wanted to tell her that he'd gotten married in Las Vegas over the weekend. There hadn't been time for a real wedding, he said. He and his bride had only been able to take a couple of days off between films.

"When we finish this picture, we'll come for a long visit. You'll love Eve, Sis," he said, and Kyra replied she was sure she would. She was happy for him even if, for some unaccountable reason, the news of his marriage put a lump in her throat.

A couple of weeks later, Grant phoned.

"You'll never believe it," he said happily, "but I'm married! Crista's wonderful. She's in the middle of opening her shop—she makes jewelry. Beautiful stuff, you'll see. Things should ease up in the spring. We'll come for a long visit. I just know you'll love her."

Kyra said she was sure she would. And the lump rose in her throat again.

Cade didn't phone; he was off in the middle of nowhere, searching for oil, but from everything that he had—and hadn't—said the last time Kyra had seen him, she had the feeling that he, too, had fallen in love.

All the Landons had, except her.

What she'd felt for Antonio had nothing to do with love. It had to do with sex. Antonio was a sexy man and she'd wanted to sleep with him, but she hadn't been adult enough to admit it. So she'd created a dreamscape of hearts and flowers and forever-after—and she thanked her lucky stars she hadn't let herself get trapped inside it.

She was living her own life now, and if sometimes she woke in the dark with traces of dampness on her cheeks and a lump in her throat, it didn't mean a damn thing except that maybe she was coming down with a cold— or maybe she needed something more to do.

In December, the short days and endless storms made the mansion seem gloomier than ever.

"I hate this place," Kyra said to Stella one night, as the wind whistled outside.

And just like that, it came to her.

She wouldn't sell the house. It was home, despite everything, and she loved the land and the lake and the mountains that surrounded it. But the house could be changed.

The next morning, Kyra phoned her banker to be sure of just how much money she had. The answer was staggering. It was enough to tear down the mansion and rebuild it ten times over.

But that wouldn't be necessary. All she needed was an architect, a contractor and an auctioneer to sell off virtually all the mansion's massive furniture and pretentious works of art.

Her banker was surprisingly silent while she told him her plans. Her attorney was, too, when she called to say that she wanted him to use the auction's proceeds to fund a charity.

"A charity?" he choked.

"Yes. I'm not sure what kind yet—we'll just put the money into a trust or something for the time being. Can we do that?"

"Well, yes, Miss Landon, but—"

"Good," Kyra said briskly, and hung up.

Late that afternoon, head bent against yet another snowstorm, she was fighting her way uphill from the stables when she stumbled into a broad-shouldered male figure.

Her heart did a swift, double-step beat.

"Antonio?" she whispered, her voice trembling.

"Good afternoon, Miss Landon."

Kyra swallowed hard and silently cursed herself for being a fool. It was her attorney, Carl Higgins—and standing just behind him, like a Gordon setter honoring a point, was Regis Emory, her banker.

"Mr. Higgins. And Mr. Emory. What a pleasant surprise." She stomped past them toward the door of the house. "Won't you come in?"

After a few minutes of polite chitchat, Higgins got to the point.

"Miss Landon," he said with a bright smile, "Mr. Emory and I have been talking."

"Indeed," Kyra said with an equally bright smile. "About me?"

"Well, yes. We have some concerns, you see. About your plans."

Kyra didn't say anything. Higgins looked at Emory, then at her.

"We cannot imagine your father would approve."

Kyra's smile hardened. "Neither can I. But I fail to see what that has to do with anything."

"Miss Landon—" Emory, the banker, gave her a paternal smile "—isn't it foolish, such formality? Why don't we simply call you 'Kyra'?"

Kyra sat down in a wing chair and crossed her legs. "That's fine with me, Regis."

The banker's false smile quivered at the edges. "Ah— ah, where was I?"

"I'm not sure, Regis. I think you were about to tell me that I was making a terrible mistake, planning alterations for this house and selling off my father's things."

"Ah, well . . ."

"And you, Carl," Kyra said, turning to the attorney, "were going to say that my father would never approve of my using the money from the sale to fund a charity. Isn't that right?"

Emory and Higgins exchanged a swift look, and then Higgins cleared his throat.

"Kyra, my dear," he said, "we know the past months have been a strain for you. You are not yourself, and—"

"On the contrary. I am very much myself, Carl."

"What we suggest is that you put yourself in our hands." His smile was patronizing enough to make Kyra's teeth ache. "We can understand your wish to make some changes in your life. Perhaps what you need is a vacation."

"Thank you for your advice, but I've already had one."

"Is that what you were doing in Venezuela?" Emory said. "You never did explain why I had to wire you money a few months ago."

"No. I never did. And I'm not going to." Kyra rose and regarded them both coolly. "Now, if that's all...?"

"Kyra, surely you can see our only concern is for your best interests."

"What I can see is that your concern is for what Charles Landon would want."

"Dearest Kyra—"

"On second thought, I would much prefer it if you'd call me Miss Landon."

"Kyra—Miss Landon—as your father's representatives, we must advise you against destroying his home and selling off his property!"

"It isn't his home," Kyra said. "Nor is it his property. It's mine. And if you two can't understand that and see yourselves as my representatives instead of his, I'll replace you." Head high, she marched to the library door. "Good day, gentlemen. I'm sure you can find your own way out."

It didn't really surprise her when the phone rang a couple of hours later. It was a conference call from Zach and Grant, who stumbled through some inconsequential small talk before getting to the point.

Was it true that she was tearing down the mansion, selling off everything in it, and giving all her money away?

Kyra sighed. "I'm not tearing the house down," she said, "but I am planning renovations. And I'm not going to sell everything—whatever stuff you want, you're more than welcome to. And no, I'm not giving all my money away. I'm only designating the profits from the sale of the furnishings to a charity."

"What charity?" Grant said.

A scholarship fund for underprivileged Native American children, Kyra almost said. Instead, she frowned. Where had that idea come from?

"I'm—I'm not sure yet. Besides, what does it matter?"

Zach cleared his throat. What mattered, he said, was her. Had she really thought this through?

Yes, Grant added. Was she sure this was what she wanted to do?

Kyra sighed. "I'm absolutely certain." Her brothers began talking at the same time. "Look," she said, "it's almost Christmas. Why don't you guys fly out here for a couple of days? I know you're busy, but this way I can meet your wives. And I'll answer all your questions."

"Good," Grant said briskly. "And then we'll decide what's the best course of action."

"No," Kyra said gently but very firmly. "No, Grant, we won't decide anything. I've already reached a decision. But I'm more than willing to try to make you understand it."

After Kyra hung up, Grant and Zach stayed on the line.

"Something's wrong," Zach said.

Grant agreed. "She's confused. She misses Father."

"Yeah." Zach sighed. "Well, we knew she would. She loved the old man a lot. Look, I've got a number somewhere for Cade. I'll call him."

"Fine. Tell him to meet us in Denver next week. Hell, we can't let our baby sister screw up her life."

Zach and Eve, Grant and Crista, all flew into Denver on the same day. It was snowing—there was nothing unusual in that. What was unusual was that it was Kyra who met them at the gate, not the Landon chauffeur.

After lots of hugs and kisses, Grant looked around.

"Where's Jeffers?" he said.

Kyra, who was busy getting to know her new sisters-in-law, gave him a distracted smile.

"He retired. Didn't I mention it?"

"No. No, you didn't. Who'd you hire in his place?"

"No one," Kyra said. She leaned toward Crista and touched her index finger to one of Crista's delicate silver earrings. "Did you make these? I just adore them!"

"Well," Zach said, "never mind. We'll hire a new chauffeur while we're here. In the meanwhile, where's the limousine driver?"

"No," Kyra said, "you won't hire a chauffeur. And you're looking at the limousine driver."

Zach and Grant stared at each other in horror. "You mean, you—you've been doing your own driving?" Grant sputtered.

"Why on earth not? I've had a license for years."

"Well, during the summer I suppose it's okay. But in snow, on these roads..."

"The Land Rover has four-wheel drive."

"Yes, but—"

"Oh, Grant." Crista looped her arm through her husband's. "Stop sounding so stuffy! Kyra's not a baby."

"Of course she isn't," Zach said in a conciliatory tone. "It's just that you girls don't know what it's like driving on these roads in winter."

"Kyra grew up here," Eve said as she took her husband's arm. "Just like you guys. As for us 'girls'..." Her delicate brows lifted. "Personally, I don't see a girl in sight, darling. I see three perfectly capable grown women."

Kyra laughed. She was, she could see, going to adore her sisters-in-law.

But Grant and Zach exchanged glances that said maybe they should have left their wives at home.

Cade and Angelica flew in the next day, grubby and exhausted from a seemingly endless flight from Europe that had involved half a dozen layovers.

"We got married during the last one," Cade said with a boyish grin. "Heck, there was nothing else to keep us occupied."

Angelica gave him a gentle punch in the arm. "I've no idea why I love this man," she said to her new family.

"Probably because I'm the only guy who'd ever put up with you," Cade said, grinning even harder. "And because I love you so much you took pity on me."

Everyone laughed, including Kyra. But her laugh caught in her throat. She had loved like this once, so deeply that everything else was unimportant.

No. No, it wasn't true. Your own self-respect was always important. Besides, she hadn't loved Antonio. She'd only thought she did.

Suddenly, horribly, her eyes filled with tears. Kyra pulled a tissue from her pocket and jammed it to her eyes.

"Coming down with a cold, Squirt?" Cade asked.

"Yes," she sniffed, and he smiled.

But she hadn't fooled her sisters-in-law.

"Kyra's unhappy," Eve whispered to Zach late that night.

"She's depressed," Crista murmured to Grant at almost the same moment.

"She's terribly sad," Angelica told Cade, "and I'd bet it has something to do with a man."

The next morning, after unwrapping the presents under the tree in the library, Eve, Crista and Angelica made seemingly casual exits. Zach, Grant and Cade sat down and faced Kyra.

"Well," Grant said.

"Well," Zach said.

Cade cleared his throat.

Kyra sighed. "Okay," she said, "here it is in a nutshell." She took a breath. "I hate this house."

Her brothers looked as if she'd told them she was running off to join a circus.

"Hate it?" Grant shook his head. "Don't be silly. You love it!"

"I hate it," she said patiently. "I always have."

"But—but you never said—"

"Of course I didn't! I was stuck here. And then, after Father died, I knew you guys had this happy image of me waiting on the hearth like a cocker spaniel."

Cade frowned. "Okay. Okay, so you don't like the house. But don't you think you're being a little hasty, selling off all the old ma . . . all Father's stuff?"

Kyra looked at him. "Why?"

"What do you mean, why? Because—because you'll regret it, that's why. Because he loved these things and they're yours now. Don't you want them around you for remembrance?"

Kyra walked to the fireplace and poked at the logs blazing on the grate.

"Actually, I've got enough bad memories of Father to last a lifetime. I'm hoping that changing this house will make some of them go away so I can begin to remember some of the good ones."

Her brothers stared at her in silence. "What bad memories?" Zach finally said.

Kyra tossed the poker onto the hearth. "Oh, for heaven's sake, are you all still so blind? I know how miserably our father treated you guys!"

"But he adored you," Grant said.

"Yes. He adored me—at the expense of all the rest of you! And he wouldn't have adored me half so much if I'd ever stood up to him and told him what I really thought."

"Kyra," Cade said, moving toward her, "baby—"

"I am *not* a baby, any more than I was Father's angel! I just pretended I was his oh-so-sweet girl because it helped keep the peace." She glared at all three of her brothers. "Well, he's gone now. I loved him in spite of himself, I suppose. But there's no need for me to keep pretending anymore, is there?" She put her hands on her hips. "I don't mind hanging on to the house—every family needs a place to think of as home. But I'm going to bring some light and warmth and happiness into this horrible place and if you guys have a problem with that, to heck with all of you!''

Silence fell across the room. Then, one by one, Kyra's brothers began to grin.

''Well, I'll be damned,'' Cade finally said, and in a second the four Landons were in each other's arms. When they broke apart, Kyra smiled.

''You know what? I almost feel like a full member of the Deadeye Defenders.''

Zach looked at her. ''You remember all that?''

Kyra held up her hand in the secret Deadeye sign. ''Deadeye Defenders never lose,'' she said, grinning.

The brothers smiled. ''Membership it is,'' Cade said.

Kyra smiled. ''With full voting rights? This country's into sexual equality, in case you hadn't heard.''

Her brothers laughed. ''Okay,'' Grant said, ''hold out your right hand.''

Kyra did and the Landons clasped hands in what had once been the brothers' childhood ritual.

''Cross my heart and hope to die, join the ghosts up in the sky, it's the truth and not a lie, Deadeye Defenders never cry,'' they intoned.

''We hereby declare you a Deadeye,'' Zach said solemnly.

''Thank you,'' Kyra said just as solemnly.

They all smiled and stepped apart again. Cade cleared his throat.

''Being a full member of the Deadeyes gives you certain obligations,'' he said briskly. ''For instance, you'll have to resolve a difference of opinion between my gorgeous wife and me.''

Kyra looked at him. ''About what?''

He smiled as if what he was about to say was too ridiculous for words.

''You'll laugh.''

"Try me."

"Well, Angelica somehow got it into her head that you'd taken a tumble for some guy and ended up getting your heart broken."

Kyra gave a snort of indignation. "That's ridiculous."

"Yeah. That's what I told her."

"I haven't taken a tumble for anybody."

"Of course not."

"And if I had—if I had, I certainly wouldn't have let him break my heart!"

Cade nodded. "That's what I told Angelica. I said, hey, my sister's no jerk. She'd never let some guy do that to her."

"You're damned right I wouldn't. Why—why..."

Kyra's gaze flew over her brothers' smiling faces. It was so good to have them here. But no one, not even her wonderful brothers, could fill the hole in her heart that had been there since she'd lost Antonio.

Without warning, a sob burst from her throat.

"Hey," Zach said, "hey, Sis..."

She swung away, but not in time. She was weeping, and she couldn't seem to stop.

Behind her, the Landon brothers threw stunned looks at each other. All three of them took a step toward Kyra, then drew back.

After what seemed a long, long while, she took a deep breath and turned to face them.

"Sorry," she said as she saw their stricken expressions. "I—I didn't mean that to happen."

Grant pulled a white linen handkerchief from his jacket pocket and handed it to her. She nodded, wiped her eyes, blew her nose, sank down on the edge of the stone hearth, and gave Cade a smile so wistful it made his throat tighten.

"Angelica was right," she said. "I did fall in love. It just—it didn't work out."

The questions came hard and fast. Who was the man? Where had she met him? What had gone wrong?

Kyra held up her hand. "I won't go into details. What happened, happened. The bottom line is that I—I fell for a man who—who didn't really love me."

Grant's face grew dark. "What do you mean, he didn't love you?"

"Just that. He—he was attracted to me, but we—we just couldn't agree on what we expected from each other."

"What did he want? Money? Property?" Zach's hands balled into fists. "Who is this bastard, Kyra?"

"I won't discuss it, Zach. I appreciate your concern, but this is my life. I messed it up and I'll do whatever needs doing to get over it."

"Yeah." Cade's voice was grim. "You really look like you're getting over it, dammit. No wonder you've gotten so skinny."

Kyra laughed and blew her nose again. "Now you sound like Stella. I haven't gotten skinny. Really. I've just been busy. I'm taking classes, I agreed to run the Art Exhibit—"

"Did this guy take advantage of you?" Grant demanded. When Kyra flushed, he cursed under his breath. "Dammit, tell me who he is, Kyra. I'll take him apart!"

"I slept with him," she said, her eyes daring him to object. "But it was my idea as much as his. It was because I loved him. Because I thought I loved him. Because..."

Oh God! She started crying again. Helplessly, Zach and Cade whipped out their handkerchiefs and handed them to her. Kyra nodded, buried her face in them, and waited until she could speak without weeping.

She looked up and gave her brothers a wobbly smile.

"I love you guys," she said. "And you needn't worry about me. I'm going to be fine."

"Yeah," Cade said.

"Right," Zach agreed.

"Sure," Grant added.

Everyone in the room knew it was a lie.

In April, the first signs of spring began to appear. Crocuses poked their heads through patches of snow; the cold wind changed to a soft breeze that bore the faintest scent of green, growing things.

Grant phoned his brothers with news. Landon Enterprises had a buyer.

"How much?" Cade asked. "Not that I really care— from what I've seen lately, the Landon balance sheet looks no better than when we took over."

"Yeah," Zach said, "how much? We cleaned up the Triad mess and the Gordon oil stuff but now everything else is going bad."

Grant cleared his throat. "Actually, he hasn't made an offer yet."

"What you mean," Zach said, "is that we have a buyer but we haven't negotiated a price."

Grant glanced at the tall, broad-shouldered man standing at his office window, looking out at the street below.

"Well, he says he won't make an offer unless it's to all three of us in person. Look, how about if we meet at the Landon offices in Denver 10:00 a.m. next Friday? Can you guys manage that?"

"Okay," Cade said after a moment.

"Yeah," Zach said, "sure. It'll give us the chance to see Kyra again. No matter how many times I talk to her on the phone, I'm still not convinced she's all right."

Grant nodded. "I agree. She sounds too cheerful. Like somebody whistling in a graveyard."

"Exactly." Cade's voice hardened. "Hell, I'd like to get my hands on the son of a bitch who hurt her!"

Zach and Grant agreed. After a round of goodbyes, they all hung up.

Grant swung his chair around, stood, and walked toward the man at the window.

"Okay," he said pleasantly, and held out his hand. "It's a go. My brothers and I will be in Denver next Friday morning. I'm sure everything will work out as you hope, *señor*."

Antonio Rodrigo Cordoba del Rey looked at Grant Landon's outstretched hand. He would kill me if he knew what I have done to his sister, he thought, and for a moment, he felt as if a knife had twisted in his heart. But then he remembered what Kyra had done to him, the bitterness he felt whenever he thought of her, and he smiled and accepted Grant's hand.

"I am sure things will work out exactly as I hope," he said.

Grant nodded. He hoped so, too. The sooner they unloaded Landon's, the happier they'd all be. Besides, there was something about Antonio del Rey that suggested he was a man who damned near always got what he wanted.

He had no way of knowing that what Antonio wanted now was revenge.

CHAPTER ELEVEN

ANTONIO arrived for the meeting early, by design.

He ignored the flustered receptionist's assurance that she was sure the Landons would be arriving at any moment, and asked to be shown to the boardroom, where the meeting was to take place.

It was important to his plan to have the high ground. There would be a psychological advantage, however slight, in greeting Kyra's brothers on their own territory instead of being greeted by them.

And Antonio wanted every advantage he could manage. It would heighten the pleasure of what came next.

He was surprised at the coldly elaborate architecture and furnishings of the massive room. He had expected something simpler after seeing Grant's New York law office, but then, Grant had partners. Perhaps they didn't share the Landon taste for pretension. This room was meant to impress if not intimidate.

But Antonio was not easily impressed, and he couldn't remember the last time he'd been intimidated. In fact, the room had just the opposite effect. It made him remember, with icy clarity, Kyra's rejection of him and everything he was.

His mouth narrowed. He had been consumed with anger the day she'd left him, but as time passed, that anger had turned into a hard knot lodged in his belly. He knew it was there, like a slow-acting poison, eating away at his gut, and there was nothing he could do to purge himself of it.

And then one day, one of his attorneys had stumbled across the solution without even being aware of it. No one knew what had happened between him and Kyra Landon except, perhaps, Dolores, who was smart enough to ask no questions.

Antonio had been at a meeting in Atlanta that had ended, as such meetings often did, with suggestions for new ventures. Milton Chaffee had put a folder on the table. He'd said he'd come across something intriguing. There was a company for sale with holdings in a dozen different areas—manufacturing, real estate, oil and gas, even movies.

Antonio had hardly paid attention. He'd found himself less interested in new endeavors the past months; that, too, was Kyra's fault. He was so consumed with his hatred of her that anything else seemed an intrusion.

But he'd tuned in enough to hear Chaffee say that the company was showing signs of fatigue.

"It's being neglected, Antonio. I can't get a handle on all the ins and outs but the bottom line seems to be that the original owner was deeply involved in running it. But his heirs—his sons—don't believe in getting their hands dirty."

Antonio had tried to curb his impatience. "Is there a point to all this, Milton?"

Chaffee smiled. "I had a business prof once, used to call it the 'Spoiled Brat' syndrome. The old man works his ass off, makes a zillion bucks so his kids will have a better life than he had and then it turns out he's done such a good job that his la-di-da offspring are only interested in *la dolce vita*."

"Milton..."

"Okay, okay. Look, the company's for sale for a fat asking price, but it's developing big problems on half a dozen fronts. A company this size in private ownership needs an interested guy at the helm, know what I mean?"

"And? Why should we want to buy it—I assume that is what you're leading up to, is it not? If the cost is high and the problems are great ..."

Chaffee leaned closer. "I've got contacts, Antonio. The heirs want to sell so bad they'd kiss the buyers."

"So? Wait until they drop the price a couple of million dollars."

"My contacts assure me they'd do better than that with some prompting." Chaffee winked. "They also tell me that the production company this outfit owns out in La La Land is gonna hit with a low-budget flick that will make the big studios drool. There's even a rumor that it has a rinky-dink oil operation in Texas ready to bring in a well that'll make the commodities market go wild."

"Surely the heirs know this?"

"They never even go into the office, Antonio. I'm telling you, they want out."

It was the sort of deal that would once have fascinated Antonio. Now, he could only think of how little he wanted to do with fools such as the brothers Chaffee was describing, men born to wealth and privilege who didn't know how to husband it while others suffered through life.

He rose to his feet. "Thank you for the information, Milton, but I am not interested."

"Antonio, let me run the figures past you. We could take it for a song, squeeze the current owners until they cried for mercy."

"I do not do business that way," Antonio said coldly.

"Don't squeeze 'em, then! We could still buy Landon Enterprises for a fraction of what it's worth and—"

"Landon Enterprises?" Antonio had said, his face suddenly white.

"Yeah. Based in Colorado. Will you at least listen?"

Antonio had listened. Then he'd taken Chaffee's folder and shoved it into his briefcase.

"I will think about it," he'd said in a way that meant the discussion was over.

Back on San Sebastian, he'd spent days going through the Landon figures and nights thinking about how he might use them.

The company, once as rich as Croesus, was faltering. Chaffee seemed to be right; Landon's had been led by one man. Now, Charles Landon's sons were letting their father's empire fall into disarray. There was little in the files about them but Antonio had no difficulty picturing what they were: spoiled brats who had never quite grown up, accustomed to privilege and without any thought of ever living without it.

Like their sister.

Was Kyra heir to Landon Enterprises, too? It seemed likely. Her brothers were probably running it without her presence—what would a woman like Kyra know of business?

Antonio paced the gardens at San Sebastian while he tried to decide what to do next. He could ride in like a knight on a charger, save Landon Enterprises by offering an infusion of cash at low interest or by buying it at the ridiculously high asking price.

Or he could do just the opposite—bring Kyra and her brothers to their knees.

What would happen to her precious expectations when she realized that the man she'd treated with such contempt could save her or savage her with the stroke of a pen?

It was a cruel plan. A malevolent one. And he was not proud of it.

Yet he had known instantly that he would do it.

Had there been time, he'd have done more groundwork, instructed Chaffee to start some carefully

placed rumors about Landon's imminent collapse. But
time was a luxury he didn't have. If word about the
possible oil strike or successful movie got out, others
would be interested in buying Landon's, too.

Antonio couldn't let that happen. He wanted Kyra's
family, and Kyra, at his mercy. And so he'd made a few
calls to some people he knew, gotten some papers
together. Then he'd phoned Grant Landon and set up
an appointment.

And now he was here, in this pretentious boardroom,
about to meet with what he had already begun thinking
of as the Landon Spoiled Brats.

Antonio frowned. Except that the one brother he'd
already met, Grant, hadn't been what he'd expected.
Grant seemed pleasant and quick-witted, and he had a
handshake that suggested he'd done more with his life
than lie in the sun. His law firm was small but Antonio
had learned it was highly placed, with an assortment of
solid, demanding clients.

"Antonio. Sorry we weren't here to greet you."

Antonio turned from the window. Grant stood in the
doorway with two men who had to be his brothers. And
there was a woman standing just behind them.

His heart rose into his throat. Kyra, he thought,
Kyra . . .

But it wasn't Kyra. It was a polite young secretary,
carrying a small tape recorder.

Antonio shook his head. "This will be a closed
meeting," he said sharply.

The Landons looked at him, their eyes narrowing.
Then Grant nodded and motioned the young woman
from the room.

"All right," he said. "We can rough out the preliminaries and go on record later." The door shut and
he and his brothers moved forward. "Antonio del Rey,
these are my brothers, Cade and Zach."

The handshakes were perfunctory. Cade and Zach looked at each other. What was with this guy? He had requested this meeting; now he was behaving as if he'd sooner have been anyplace but here.

Everyone took a seat at the mahogany conference table. Grant cleared his throat, launched into some opening remarks, and Antonio spoke right across them.

"I would prefer to get directly to the point," he said. And without any preliminaries, he made his purchase offer.

There was a silence, and then the three Landons began to laugh.

"You're kidding," Zach said.

Antonio shook his head. "I am quite serious."

"Well, then, the discussion is over. There's not a way in the world we'd—"

Antonio opened his briefcase, tossed papers on the table. The brothers looked at each other, then reached for the papers. There was another silence, and then Cade looked up, his handsome face white with barely suppressed rage.

"What kind of crap is this, del Rey?"

"It is exactly what it seems to be, Señor Landon," Antonio said coldly. "Landon Enterprises owes money to a number of banks. It is unfortunate that they have all chosen to call in their loans at the same time."

"They can't do that," Zach growled.

Antonio shrugged. "Perhaps, and perhaps not. But while your attorneys and theirs argue over the details, word will get out that Landon Enterprises is on the brink of financial collapse."

"This is a holdup," Grant snarled. "You son of a bitch, you know you can't get away with this!"

"I know that you will not be able to sell the company for a dime on the dollar, once people begin to talk." Antonio smiled. "My offer will look more than ac-

ceptable to you then, gentlemen, but it will not exist.''
His smile faded. ''I will be at the Hilton until this time
tomorrow. You have twenty-four hours to reach a
decision.''

It was Cade who went for him first, launching himself
over the table with both hands extended. Zach and Grant
grabbed him and wrestled him back.

''Don't,'' Grant said, his face white and his eyes on
Antonio's. ''The bastard isn't worth it.''

''Why?'' Zach said as Antonio picked up his briefcase
and strode to the boardroom door. ''Just tell us why,
dammit!''

Antonio looked at him, his face expressionless.

''Why not?''

Zach shook his head. ''If I didn't know better, I'd say
this was some kind of vendetta.'' He scowled. ''Is it?
Did you have dealings with our father in the past? Is
that what this is all about?''

It was, Antonio knew, the perfect moment. And he
made the most of it; he took his time answering, looking
from one furious face to the other, and then he smiled.

''Be sure and tell your sister that Antonio Rodrigo
Cordoba del Rey sends his regards.''

Antonio stepped into the hall and let the door swing
shut after him.

They decided to tell Kyra nothing. She wasn't involved
in the business end of things, Zach said. Why should
they drag her into such a sleazy mess?

Cade agreed. As for the money—it wasn't as if they
needed it personally. It was all going to charity anyway;
they'd agreed on that months ago.

Grant said they were both right. Hell, they could give
Landon's away, for all it mattered. It was just the prin-
ciple of the thing, the del Rey guy coming to see him in

New York like a perfectly sane human being and then turning out to be evil incarnate.

The brothers looked at each other. As for that last crack about Kyra... How could del Rey have known her? Where could he have...? Could this be the guy who...?

No. No, their little sister would never have fallen for such a coldhearted bastard. Whatever del Rey had meant by that remark wasn't worth thinking about. Their first reaction was the right one; they would not mention Antonio del Rey to her. Why upset their baby sister?

That decision lasted as long as it took to drive to the mansion. By the time Grant flung the door open, the Landons were three sticks of dynamite with a short fuse.

Kyra was in the entry hall, arranging the first of the season's white daffodils in a vase.

"Hi," she said, looking up. "How'd it go? Did you guys sell—"

"Who in hell is Antonio del Rey?" Cade demanded, while Zach and Grant glowered at her.

Kyra stared at her brothers blankly. "What?"

"You heard what he said!" Zach stalked forward, his arms crossed over his chest. "What have you got to do with some two-bit Latin bastard named Antonio del Rey?"

"I don't—I don't understand."

"He's our buyer," Grant said tightly. "Or he'd like to be. But we'd rather give the company away than sell to that son of a bitch."

Kyra felt behind her for support. Her hand closed on the edge of the hall table.

"Antonio wants to buy Landon's?" she said shakily.

The brothers shot knowing looks at each other. Antonio, she'd called that bastard. Antonio!

"Who is he?" Cade said. "And how does he know you?"

Kyra moistened her lips. Could her brothers hear her heart pounding? Could they tell that her legs might give out and drop her to the floor at any minute?

"Antonio is—is here? In Denver?"

"He's at the Hilton, offering to slice out our hearts while he sends you his regards." Grant's eyes fixed on hers. "And we want to know why."

"He's a..." Kyra's gaze swept desperately over the three angry male faces. "He's—he's a man, that's all."

"A man." Zach laughed coldly as he looked at his brothers. "He's a man, she says. He hates our guts, he tells us to give our little sister a hug and a kiss, and she says he's—"

"What—what exactly did he say? About—about me?"

"It wasn't what he said. It was the way he said it." Grant's mouth twisted. "Did you meet him on that cruise you took?"

"The cruise you never thought of mentioning to us until it was over," Cade snapped.

"Yeah," Zach said, "that cruise you went off on without a damned word. Is that where you picked him up?"

Kyra's spine stiffened. "I didn't pick him up."

"What did you do, then? Because it doesn't take a genius to tell the guy hates you big time!"

Take it easy, Kyra told herself, just take it easy. Take deep breaths. Good. Good.

"We're waiting, Kyra. Why's he got it in for you?"

"I—I suppose you could say we're not—we're not each other's favorite human beings," she ventured cautiously.

"Yeah," Cade retorted, "we figured that. Now we want to know the reason."

Kyra's chin lifted. "It's none of your business."

Cade's brows shot to his hairline. "What do you mean, it's none of our business? Everything about you is our business. Father's gone now. Who'll watch out for you if not us?"

"I'll watch out for me!"

"What kind of answer is that?"

"An honest one."

"Listen here, Squirt—"

"I'm tired of listening! And don't call me Squirt!"

"Cade. Zach." Grant stepped forward and put a hand on each of his brother's shoulders. "Let me talk to her alone."

Both brothers blew out their breaths, glared at Kyra one last time, and stalked from the room. Grant waited until the door shut, and then he turned to his sister with a smile that set her teeth on edge.

"Kyra, dear..."

"Oh, for pity's sake, Grant!" Kyra flung her hands onto her hips. "Don't start treating me as if I were five years old! And don't waste your breath. I am not telling you anything."

"I certainly have the right to ask if this man is a danger to you." Grant said sharply.

"No," she said, "he's no danger to me."

"But you were... involved with him?"

She nodded. "Yes."

Grant nodded, too. "He's the one, isn't he?"

She didn't have to ask what he meant. The seconds flew by and then she gave a deep, deep sigh.

"Yes," she said, "he's the one."

She saw Grant's hands knot into fists and she sprang forward and clutched his forearms. The muscles were knotted, hard as rocks under her fingers.

"You're to stay out of this," she said.

"Stay out of it? Your pal dragged us into it!"

"Antonio is—he's trying to get back at me through you. And I'm the one who has to put a stop to it."

"See him, you mean?" Grant shook his head. "Absolutely not!"

"Don't be ridiculous! You can't tell me what to do."

Grant's jaw shot forward. "I forbid you to go within ten feet of Antonio del Rey."

"You forbid me?"

"Yeah. That's right." Grant folded his arms. "Is that clear, Kyra? You are not to go near this man."

Kyra forced a smile to her lips. "All right."

"Don't just say all right. You'd better mean it."

"Have I a choice? I won't go near him, Grant. Okay?"

Grant nodded. "Okay," he said, and then he shook his head and pulled her into his arms. "We know what's best, Sis. We love you."

"I know you do." Kyra drew back. "Look, this has been pretty upsetting. Would you mind if I passed on lunch?"

Grant nodded sympathetically. "Sure. Go on to your room, lie down for a couple of hours. And don't worry about a thing. We'll take care of this character for you."

Kyra smiled. "I know you will."

She threw Grant a kiss, left the room, and closed the door after her. She smiled blithely at Cade and Zach, then made her way upstairs.

As soon as she heard the library door shut, she flew down the stairs, grabbed a jacket from the hall, and raced out the back door to the garage.

It was easy getting Antonio's suite number. Kyra used a trick she'd learned from a detective novel. She scribbled his name on a hotel envelope, sealed it, and asked that it be left in Señor del Rey's box. The clerk turned, put it into the appropriately numbered slot, and she was in business.

Her mouth was dry as she knocked at the door to his suite. Her heart was hammering, too. With anger, she reminded herself, not with anything else. To think she'd wasted a moment of her life, thinking she loved this man! To think she'd ever devoted a minute to wishing she were still with him, on his island...

The door opened.

"Yes?" Antonio said coldly. "What is it, please? I did not order..."

She saw his eyes darken with realization and she began to tremble. How could the sight of him, how could just looking into his sapphire eyes, make her feel this way?

She took a deep breath. "Hello, Antonio," she said. "May I come in?"

"*Sí*. Of course." She could see him stiffening, recovering his poise. Good. She had caught him off guard; that would be some small advantage. "Come in. I—I did not expect you, Kyra."

"I know that." She waited until he'd shut the door and then turned to him, her eyes cold. "You thought you could bring my brothers to heel and I'd let you get away with it."

Antonio walked to the small bar across the room. He took a bottle of brandy from the tray and poured himself a drink. His hands were trembling; he could only hope Kyra had not noticed. How could the sight of her still move him so? She was even more beautiful then he remembered, more beautiful than when she haunted his dreams....

He took a deep breath. "Would you like a drink?"

"I didn't come here for a sociable chat, Antonio." He turned as she came toward him, her small, elegant face lifted in defiance. "I came to tell you that your scheme won't work. You can't use my brothers to get back at me."

"Have they explained the situation to you?"

"They've told me enough. I know that you want to bring Landon Enterprises to its knees. What I don't quite understand is why."

He took a mouthful of brandy, swallowed it, and smiled at her over the rim of the glass.

"I think you do."

"I don't. What do you hope to gain?"

He smiled unpleasantly. "You are pleading with me not to destroy your brothers, aren't you?"

Kyra laughed. "Do I sound as if I'm pleading?"

He frowned. It was true, she didn't. But that was why she'd come here, surely—to beg him not to ruin her brothers, perhaps even herself.

"Are you really still so angry that you didn't win, Antonio? Angry enough to behave like a spoiled child?"

His face darkened. "I? I, a spoiled child?"

"I wouldn't do what you wanted so you decided to get even. Isn't that what this is all about?"

Antonio slammed down his glass and walked toward her, his eyes flashing.

"One of us is spoiled, Kyra, but it is surely not I!"

"Oh, come on!" Kyra glared at him. "You wanted me to agree to let you control my life and I said I wouldn't do it. So you sat around and brooded and then you came up with this idea, a way you thought you could control my brothers' lives instead."

"This is not a matter of control," he said coldly. "It is a matter of learning that one's expectations are not always what one hopes they will be."

"Well, you're right about that. You see, you can't ruin my brothers. They don't need the Landon money." She folded her arms. "Zach, Cade and Grant made their own way in the world. Whatever they get from the sale of Landon Enterprises will go to charity."

"To charity?"

She smiled coolly at his puzzled expression. "It's their way of throwing off the yoke of slavery."

"I do not understand."

"No. You wouldn't. You're a tyrant yourself, a domineering, coldhearted, controlling—"

She gasped as his hands closed on her shoulders. "Watch your mouth, Kyra. I will not permit you to insult me."

"You came to Denver to insult me! To humiliate me! As far as I'm concerned, that gives me the right to say whatever I damned please. This is a free country, Antonio. You can't play at being emp—"

His mouth fell on hers. It was a hard, angry kiss, yet more proof of his need to dominate, but when it came to this, Antonio had always dominated her. He had always been the victor in this most intimate of games because by taking, he also gave.

And he was giving now. His kiss was changing, going from hard and angry to sweet and tender. "*Querida*," he whispered against her mouth, or was it only that she longed to hear the word from his lips? It didn't matter. She couldn't help her response, the way her arms were winding around his neck, the way she was lifting herself to him, fitting her body and her lips to his....

They broke apart, both of them breathing hard and flushed with emotion. Antonio swallowed, then turned and walked to where he had left his glass. He picked it up, put it to his lips, and drank down what remained of the brandy.

"It will not work," he said. His voice was cold. "This little display is—amusing. But I will not change my mind, Kyra. Your brothers will accept my offer or the company will fail in bankruptcy. The decision is theirs."

Kyra stood staring at him, at that rigid back and that too-proud angle of that dark head, and suddenly she gave a cry of fury and rushed toward him. Startled,

Antonio spun around and caught her as she began pounding her fists against his chest.

"You bastard!" she panted. "How can you do this? It isn't as if you cared whether I stayed with you or not. It isn't as if you loved me. I was the one who made a fool of myself, falling in love with a man who didn't give a damn for me! I was the idiot who tried and tried to explain!"

"To explain what? That you loved me?" Antonio caught her wrists and immobilized her hands against his chest. "Do not lie to me, Kyra. I was offering you my heart and my name and all you could think of were your precious expectations, the pointless accident of your birth that would forever keep you and your family from deigning to accept a man like me!"

"Are you crazy? Why wouldn't my family accept a man like you? Someone who's brave and gentle and generous and—and—"

Her mouth snapped shut, but it was too late. Antonio's eyes darkened.

"Do you really think those things of me?" he said softly.

"No," Kyra said furiously as she tried to jerk her hands free. "Of course not! Let go of me, dammit! I thought my father was impossible, trying to mold me to suit some image, but you're worse! Now you're accusing me of—of coming here to entice you into backing off."

"That kiss, then, was freely given?"

"Yes, damn you! Not that I don't regret it—"

Antonio kissed her again, his mouth moving gently against hers. Kyra held back, telling herself she must not respond, but it was like trying to stop the sun from rising in the morning. She gave a little sob and leaned into his embrace, her hands clutching at his shirt.

Antonio looked down at her when the kiss ended. Gently, he brushed his knuckles over her cheek.

"What is this, about being forced to fit some image?"

"It doesn't matter. Oh hell. Yes, it does matter! It's what my father used to do. It's what you wanted to do, telling me that you'd only want me if I'd agree to—to obey your rules and let you treat me like some hothouse orchid!"

Antonio's eyes narrowed. "I never asked that of you, *querida*. Why would I, when your spirit is so precious to me?"

"Well, what else were you asking me?"

"I just told you. I was asking you to be my wife, despite the differences in our backgrounds."

Kyra went very still. That *was* what he'd said, she suddenly thought, and her heart missed a beat.

"You mean—you were proposing to me?" she whispered.

A muscle knotted in Antonio's cheek. "Yes."

"Oh, Antonio. I didn't—I thought..."

His hands swept into her hair and he tilted her face up to his.

"And what you said a few moments ago..." He took a breath. "Did you truly say that you loved me?"

Kyra felt the swift rush of happy tears rise in her eyes.

"You foolish man," she answered softly. "I not only love you, I adore you. But I couldn't agree to be a good, obedient, docile cow. And I thought that was what you wanted."

Antonio laughed as his arms went around her. "A cow? What a thought, *querida*. An Arabian, perhaps, high-spirited and beautiful, but a cow? Never!"

He drew her close and kissed her again, long and deeply, and then he smiled into her eyes.

"So," he said gruffly, "you will agree to become Señora Antonio del Rey, yes?"

Kyra smiled back at him. "I will agree to become Señora Kyra del Rey. *Sí*."

"And to love me for the rest of your life?"

"Only if you make the same promise."

"*Sí, mi amor*. I will love you till the end of time—but you must not turn into a cow. That, I could not bear."

Kyra laughed and wrapped her arms around him.

"I should warn you, my brothers are going to need some fast talking to calm them down. They're a little upset at the thought that you took advantage of me."

Antonio chuckled. "I will explain to them that you gave me no choice, that you dragged me into your bed."

He bent and kissed her again and again until her mouth was sweetly swollen, and then he smiled into her eyes.

"I will tell you what we must do, *querida*. We must go to your brothers and assure them that I am not a pirate come to steal their company. And that we wish to set a date for our wedding." He smiled. "That will calm them, *sí*?"

Kyra caught her breath as Antonio lifted her into his arms.

"But first," he said, his voice husky, "first, we will make up for the weeks and months we have wasted. Does that live up to your expectations, *mi amor*?"

Kyra's answer was in her kiss.

EPILOGUE

EARLY morning sunlight streamed through the arched windows of the Landon mansion, spilling golden brilliance over the oyster white walls and brightly colored rya rugs that were scattered over the bleached-oak floors.

In the room that had so long ago been his, Cade Landon's arm tightened around the woman nestled beside him. She sighed and moved closer to him; her tumble of fiery copper curls brushed softly against his cheek.

Cade blinked his eyes open. He lay still, getting his bearings.

It was a long time since he'd awakened in this room. For just a moment, the old feelings of childhood swept over him—the pent-up anger, the unhappiness, the despair...

And then he became aware of Angelica lying in his arms, of her warmth and her scent, and all the memories were swept away. Carefully, so as not to wake her, he rose up on his elbow and gazed down at her.

A smile curved across his mouth. She was so beautiful. So wonderful. And she was his—his partner, his companion, his lover...

His wife.

Gently, he reached out and stroked the copper curls from her cheek.

It was still a wonder to him, not just that he had found her, but how she had changed his life. Until Angelica, his pleasure had been measured by the exotic places he'd been and the beautiful women he'd found in them, and by the rushing geysers of black gold he coaxed from deep inside the earth.

Now, his wife was all the pleasure he needed, all he would ever need. He could not imagine life without her, without her sweetness and her passion. He smiled a little. And without her fiery temper.

"Good morning."

Angelica's beautiful green eyes were open; her mouth was curved into the gentlest of smiles. A feeling so potent it made his throat tighten swept over him, and he took her into his arms almost fiercely, claiming her lips with his.

After a long moment, he drew back. Angelica's face was flushed; she smiled as she linked her hands behind his neck.

"Mmm," she sighed, "what a nice way to start the day."

Cade grinned. "I'm better than an alarm clock, am I?"

Her laugh was soft and wicked, "Especially since I never get alarmed."

"Angel," he said, "I've been thinking..." He hesitated, then took a deep breath. "You know that project we've been considering in Kuwait?"

Angelica gave a mocking sigh of distress. "That's what happens when you're an old married couple. Here I am, in my husband's arms, and all he can think of is bus—"

Cade laughed and kissed her to silence. Then he drew back and looked at her.

"What if we passed on Kuwait and took up that Alaskan offer?"

"For you to head up that company? But—but you'd have to stay in one place, Cade, and you've never wanted to."

"Oh, I don't know." He was trying to sound casual, despite the knot growing in his gut. "It might be nice to settle down. Build a house, put down roots..."

Angelica's eyes widened. "You? Put down roots?"

"Well, yeah. A guy should put down roots before he starts a family, shouldn't he?" He saw the stunned look on her face and cursed himself for dropping something like that on her without any warning. "Forget it," he said quickly. "It was just a crazy thought, and—"

"It's a wonderful thought," Angelica said, her voice breaking a little.

Cade felt his heart lift. "Do you mean it?"

"You foolish man! Of course I mean it! I love you, Cade Landon. What more could I possibly want than to settle down with you and have your babies?"

Cade kissed her, gently at first and then more passionately.

"Any objections if we start on our new project right away?" he said, smiling.

Angelica smiled back at him. "Every textbook I've ever read says that taking immediate action is the sign of a topflight CEO," she whispered.

Laughing, Cade rolled her beneath him. Without a doubt, he thought, he was the happiest, luckiest man in the world.

Down the hall, in the room he'd once thought of as a prison cell, Grant Landon woke from a deep, dreamless sleep and reached for his wife.

The bed beside him was empty. Grant shot up against the pillows, his heart hammering in his throat—and then he saw her, standing at the window, wrapped in his old flannel robe with her black hair streaming down her back like heavy silk.

Grant shoved back the blankets and got to his feet.

"Sweetheart?"

Crista turned, her beautiful face lighting with happiness when she saw him.

"Good morning," she said. "I'm sorry if I woke you."

"Darling?" Grant held out his hands. "Are you okay?"

She laughed as she put her hands into his. "Of course."

"Are you sure? Maybe you shouldn't be up so early. You need your sleep, you know. And your feet are bare. You're liable to catch a chill—"

"Grant." Crista moved closer to her husband and smiled up into his eyes. "I'm not sick, darling. I'm pregnant."

"Exactly. You're pregnant. And—"

"And I'm absolutely fine."

"Are you sure? Maybe you should ask the doctor if—"

"I did," Crista said gently. "I asked him every question you came up with, and then *you* asked him every one of those questions all over again, and the answers were always the same." She smiled. "I'm as healthy as a horse, Grant. There's not a thing in the world to worry about."

Grant frowned. "Sure. But—"

"In fact, I've never felt better in my life."

"That's fine. But—"

"Women have been having babies ever since the world began. It's not as if we invented this ourselves."

Grant sighed. "I know." His arms went around her and he drew her close. "It's just that I love you so much...."

"And I love you," Crista said. She shut her eyes and laid her head against his chest, luxuriating in the sure beat of his heart. "I don't think you'll ever know how much."

Grant drew back, putting his wife from him just enough so he could look down into her beautiful violet eyes.

"You're everything to me, Crista," he whispered. "When I think of how empty my life was without you..."

She grinned. "Remember that the next time Annie decides to pretend your favorite pair of moccasins is a doggy toy."

Grant gave a despairing sigh, but his eyes sparkled with laughter.

"Serves me right," he said, "marrying a woman who insisted a cat and a dog had to be present at the ceremony."

"They were very well behaved," Crista said, trying to keep a straight face. "Even the minister said so."

Grant gave up trying not to smile. His arms closed tightly around his wife and he gave her a long, deep kiss.

"I adore you," he murmured against her lips.

He felt her mouth curve into a smile. "I hope our son looks just like his daddy," she said.

"What an amazing coincidence. I was just thinking how nice it would be if our daughter looks like her mommy."

Crista leaned back in his arms, her smile sweetly mysterious. "Grant? What if we both could have our wish?"

"Okay, love. A girl this time, a boy next time."

"How about *both* this time?"

Grant's brow furrowed. "Both? But how...?" His eyes widened. "Oh my lord, Crista! Do you mean...?"

"We're having twins," she said with a happy laugh. "A boy and a girl. The doctor told me yesterday."

"Twins?" Grant said dumbly. "Twins?"

"Uh-huh. Two babies, darling. Two cribs. Two carriages. Two midnight feedings..."

"What wonderful news!" Grant's face was radiant with joy. "Oh, what a day this is going to be! Kyra's wedding to celebrate, and now this."

Crista looped her arms around his neck. "You know," she said softly, "we really could start celebrating right now. All by ourselves."

Grant read the sweet message in her flushed cheeks and parted lips. The thought of making love to her made his body tighten in anticipation, but he hesitated. Crista, feeling that hesitation and suspecting the reason for it, sighed and rolled her eyes.

"I'm not made of glass, Grant."

"I know. But—" Her hand moved on him and he caught his breath. "Are you certain?"

She gave a deep, happy laugh. "Absolutely. I'm healthy. And sexy. So if you really want to keep me happy…"

Laughing, Grant swept his wife into his arms. "Wicked woman," he whispered. And, as he lowered her gently to the bed and came down beside her, he knew he was the luckiest, happiest man in the world.

In the room across the hall, Zach Landon dropped a gentle kiss on his sleeping wife's tousled blond hair. Then he carefully pushed back the blankets, rose from the bed, and tiptoed into the bathroom.

It would be time to waken her soon, he thought as he stepped into the shower, but for now he wanted Eve to get as much rest as she could manage.

She wasn't feeling well, hadn't been for the past couple of weeks. And it worried the hell out of him.

Zach's gut knotted. To think of anything happening to Eve…the thought terrified him. She was his love. His life. She was everything he'd ever wanted and more than he'd dreamed of, and there wasn't a moment of the day that he didn't find himself thinking what a miracle it was that she loved him.

They'd flown in late last night from the Coast. Too late, probably, but there'd been a last-minute meeting with the production crew of Triad's next film.

Zach turned his face up to the spray and frowned. He should have put his foot down, should have said, Eve, I don't want you attending this meeting, dammit, not when you're feeling under the weather.

Not that it would have done him any good, he thought with a rueful smile. His wife was the most opinionated broad he'd ever known. You didn't "tell" her what to do, not even if you were her husband... But that was exactly what he was going to do, starting today, and she could scream bloody murder if she didn't like it!

He reached out, shut off the water, and stepped out of the shower.

There'd been some kind of bug making the rounds in L.A., one of those forty-eight-hour things that hit hard and made you feel rotten. He'd come down with it himself and spent the best part of a couple of days in groaning misery before it passed. Eve had come down with it next—but she couldn't seem to shake it. He'd begged her to see a doctor, but she'd pooh-poohed the idea.

"Really, sweetheart," she'd insisted, "I'm not sick. It's just this virus. It'll go away. You'll see."

Well, it hadn't gone away. Although it was weird— she really didn't seem ill, not as the day wore on. Still, there had to be something wrong when the woman you loved began each morning feeling nauseous and miserable and when you had to stand around feeling useless because you couldn't do a damned thing to help her. It was hell, awakening alone, knowing your wife was in the bathroom, being sick...

Zach froze.

In the bathroom? Being sick? *Every morning*?

His heart took a leap, knocked against his ribs. The bath towel fell from his suddenly nerveless fingers.

"Pregnant," he whispered. He fumbled the door open, raced across the room, stumbled to his knees beside the bed.

Eve was awake, sitting up against the pillows. Her face was pale but she was smiling.

"There you are," she said. "I missed you."

Zach's eyes swept over her beautiful face. "Eve?" He swallowed hard, reached for her hand, clasped it tightly in his. "Eve, sweetheart—are you all right?"

She nodded carefully. "I—I think I am, actually."

"No nausea?"

"No. It seems to be gone."

"You're not going to be sick?"

Eve smiled hesitantly. "I don't think so."

Zach swallowed hard. "Oh." He nodded, forced a smile to his lips. What a jerk he was! His wife had been sick for a couple of weeks and it had taken him that long to think that maybe—just maybe—it was morning sickness. And by the time he'd figured that it might be, it turned out it wasn't!

He didn't know which he felt more like doing—laughing or crying.

Eve leaned toward him and gently pushed the hair back from his forehead.

"You don't look very happy," she said softly.

"Of course I'm happy," he said quickly. His hand tightened on hers. "It killed me to know you were hurting, sweetheart. It's just that—that..."

"That what?"

He shrugged his shoulders. "Never mind."

"Come on. Tell me what you were going to say."

Zach cleared his throat. "Well, I know how dumb this sounds, darling, but—but it just occurred to me that—

I know it's ridiculous, but I found myself thinking that maybe the reason you felt lousy lately was because—because you were pregnant."

A smile as old as time curved across Eve's lips. "I am."

"I told you it was silly, but—" Zach stared at her. "What did you say?"

"I said, we're having a baby." Eve laughed softly at the look on her husband's face. "Isn't it incredible?"

"A baby," he whispered. "A baby? You and me?" With a cry of happiness, Zach folded Eve in his arms. "Oh, my love! Are you sure?"

She nodded, her face buried in his shoulder. "Positive. This time next year, you'll be a father."

A father. Him, a father. Zach's throat constricted. He wanted to tell his beautiful wife how happy he was, how happy her love had made him, but he didn't trust himself to speak. Instead, he drew back, took her face in his hands, and gave her a long, sweet kiss.

"I adore you," he breathed against her lips.

Eve laughed, though her eyes were shiny with tears of joy.

"Isn't it wonderful?"

"Wonderful," he said softly, and as he kissed her again, he thought that what was really wonderful was that he was the luckiest, happiest man in the entire world.

At noon, when the sun was a golden globe in an incredibly blue sky, a string quartet struck up the strains of "The Wedding March" and Kyra Landon appeared on the terrace overlooking the gardens, beautiful and glowing in a delicate gown of ivory lace. It had wrist-length sleeves, a long, full skirt and a sweeping train inset with tiny ivory satin roses. The neckline was just low enough to be the perfect backdrop for the diamond-

and-platinum necklace Antonio had given his bride as a wedding gift.

The silver fire of the necklace, he said, matched the color of her eyes.

Antonio, handsome and imposing in black tie, stood waiting for her at an altar bedecked with overflowing baskets of white and pink tulips. The sight of him stole Kyra's breath away. His dark hair was brushed back from his chiseled face, and his eyes, shining with love, were more blue than the spring sky.

Surrounded by her tall, handsome brothers, Kyra came down the steps and moved slowly along a path strewn with blush pink rose petals. When they reached the altar, Cade, Zach and Grant each kissed the little sister they so cherished and whispered their farewells.

Their wives, who had preceded Kyra down the aisle in gowns of palest pink, lavender and blue, tried not to cry as they took their husbands' arms.

But how could you not get misty-eyed as the beautiful bride and her handsome groom exchanged their vows? How could you not weep at the very end, when the groom raised the bride's veil to kiss her and the bride smiled into his eyes?

"I love you with all my heart, Tonio," Kyra whispered. "And I will spend my life making you happy."

"Kyra, *mia querida*," Antonio said as he took her face between his hands, "you could not make me any happier than I am at this moment. You are mine and I am yours, forever."

Kyra kissed her husband and then she drew back in his arms. She was the luckiest, happiest woman in all the world, she thought, and suddenly her throat tightened.

If only Father were here...

She looked at her brothers, and in that instant, she knew that what she saw in their eyes was what was in her own heart.

Months ago, it had seemed as if Charles Landon had left a legacy of anger and sorrow—but the power of love had changed that.

The Landon Legacy had turned out to be one of happiness and laughter, the greatest gifts a father could bestow on his children.

Maybe, just maybe, there was one last guest at the Landon wedding on this wonderful day.

For all Cade and Grant, Zach and Kyra knew, their father might be looking on, seeing the joy on the faces of his sons and his daughter, and smiling.

by Charlotte Lamb

An exciting seven-part series.

Watch for

The Sin of Envy

in

#1828 HAUNTED DREAMS

Ambrose Kerr possessed the kind of wealth and success others could only dream about—but his happiness would not be complete until he had Emilie!

Love can conquer the deadliest of

THIS TIME, FOREVER

Four years ago Darcy made a pass at heartthrob
Keir Robards. And he turned her down flat.

BUT

NOW

HE'S

BACK!

And Darcy is determined to make him pay....

#1831 FAST AND LOOSE
by Elizabeth Oldfield

Available in August wherever
Harlequin books are sold.

HARLEQUIN ◆ PRESENTS®

Look us up on-line at: http://www.romance.net

BRIDE'S BAY RESORT

UNLOCK THE DOOR TO GREAT ROMANCE AT BRIDE'S BAY RESORT

Join Harlequin's new across-the-lines series, set in an exclusive hotel on an island off the coast of South Carolina.

Seven of your favorite authors will bring you exciting stories about fascinating heroes and heroines discovering love at Bride's Bay Resort.

Look for these fabulous stories coming to a store near you beginning in January 1996.

Harlequin American Romance #613 in January
Matchmaking Baby by Cathy Gillen Thacker

Harlequin Presents #1794 in February
Indiscretions by Robyn Donald

Harlequin Intrigue #362 in March
Love and Lies by Dawn Stewardson

Harlequin Romance #3404 in April
Make Believe Engagement by Day Leclaire

Harlequin Temptation #588 in May
Stranger in the Night by Roseanne Williams

Harlequin Superromance #695 in June
Married to a Stranger by Connie Bennett

Harlequin Historicals #324 in July
Dulcie's Gift by Ruth Langan

Visit Bride's Bay Resort each month wherever Harlequin books are sold.

HARLEQUIN®

BBAYG